About the Author

Robyn Wilkinson is a resident of Brisbane, Australia. She is a secondary school teacher of English, and a graduate of the University of Queensland. Her knowledge of criminal law contributes markedly to this novel. She is married with two adult sons. Robyn is happy to be contacted at robyngwilko@gmail.com.

Trial By Error

Robyn Wilkinson

Trial By Error

Olympia Publishers
London

www.olympiapublishers.com
OLYMPIA PAPERBACK EDITION

Copyright © Robyn Wilkinson 2022

The right of Robyn Wilkinson to be identified as author of
this work has been asserted in accordance with sections 77 and 78
of the Copyright, Designs and Patents Act 1988.

All Rights Reserved

No reproduction, copy or transmission of this publication
may be made without written permission.
No paragraph of this publication may be reproduced,
copied or transmitted save with the written permission of the
publisher, or in accordance with the provisions
of the Copyright Act 1956 (as amended).

Any person who commits any unauthorised act in relation to
this publication may be liable to criminal
prosecution and civil claims for damage.

A CIP catalogue record for this title is
available from the British Library.

ISBN: 978-1-80074-057-0

This is a work of fiction.
Names, characters, places and incidents originate from the writer's
imagination. Any resemblance to actual persons, living or dead, is
purely coincidental.

First Published in 2022

Olympia Publishers
Tallis House
2 Tallis Street
London
EC4Y 0AB

Printed in Great Britain

Dedication

To my husband, Barry, my two sons, Lucas and Gregory, and my daughters-in-law, Nicola and Natsumi.

PART ONE

HOW IT ALL BEGAN

GILLIAN

She had always known this day would come. It did in almost every marriage, didn't it? It was, after all, what men were biologically programmed to do. It was just that she had never thought, even for a second, that the revelation of her replacement would come dressed as such a cliché. Although, when she stopped to think about it now, she supposed it generally did, in the form of more and more late nights at the office, even occasionally a 'work through the night', urgent call-to-arms, a just barely concealed unwillingness to have sex, the difficult household conversations, the diffidence, the more buoyant demeanour as he left their home for work.

She had heard all of this from her friend Hilary, whom she had gone through school and university with. They met for their regular after work drinks at *Felons*, a bar in the city centre favoured by the legal fraternity. Their meetings, however, once looked so forward to, so enlivening, had become tedious, almost to the point of unbearable. However their conversation started, however much she tried to steer it, when they were sufficiently lubricated it came back inevitably to the same thing. Hilary's hatred and bitterness towards her ex-husband who had left her for his, of course, younger and unsullied by pregnancies and motherhood, personal assistant. At first, Hilary was bereft and spilt countless tears, but at the same time, had assured herself that he would come back. After all, he had always said his family were everything. And how he admired his wife's fierce intelligence and the way she juggled demanding hours in the law firm where she worked with bringing up two accomplished, if distant, children. Of course, she had had help in the house. He understood when she was too tired for sex or going to that concert with him. She was nothing if not understanding and didn't ever mind him going out with a friend instead. Nor did he mind the tiny bit of weight that had crept on to her once-perfect figure, didn't ever comment on her changed penchant for Laura Ashley P&T clothes and pumps, rather than her once fitting, little black dresses and stilettos. In fact, he seemed to find the new motherly her quite adorable. Too late for regret, for changing any of this, as the realisation dawned that he was not coming back. He was, and would stay, gone. Hilary's fear had turned to despair, and then bitterness and hate, and these were a bottomless abyss.

She, Gillian, would never be reduced to this very definition of the abandoned wife as her friend had. No, she had her own cliché, the one she had always fallen back on — Don't get mad, get even. Remove the interloper. Remove the traitor. She had predicted this eventuality and she had meticulously prepared for it. At least with her and Vincent there were no children. She had never contemplated having them and she had actively prevented it from happening. Of course, Vincent had wanted them, and he had never known that the necessary little pills had their residence in the bottom drawer of her desk at work. She had never fancied her husband's affections being shared with a child. She knew what it was to compete for adoration but she had remedied that situation and would never allow herself to be in that situation again.

So, Vincent had come home from work this evening, only

a little late. He had come into the kitchen, their beautiful, natural stone kitchen in their enviable, high-ceilinged, old wool store loft, where she had marinated the swordfish and was starting on a salad. He gave her the usual peck on the cheek, reached for two wine glasses and took the chilled wine out of the refrigerator. Nothing out of the ordinary so far. But as she picked up his instantly discarded suitcoat, it caught her eye. A tiny tuft of pink angora on the front. Recognition was instant. So, his paralegal was to be her adversary, a young woman dubbed 'Fluffy' by the partner's wives, because of her predilection for a rotation of pastel coloured, figure-hugging, angora sweaters, à la Marilyn Monroe cheesecake poses, paired with pencil skirts and high heels, all showing off her enviable slim and lissom but curvaceous, young (and there was that word again) body. She felt, surprising as it may have been to others had they known, calm, focused and in control. She had silent questions. Would he actually leave her and take half of their possessions? Would this new love give him the children he would love to have? Would they grow old together, with her taking slavishly to the gym and desperately having her face filled, paralysed and stretched in order to keep his interest, while he lost his hair and grew spongy above the waist — a statement of success — and below the chin? One of life's many unfairnesses, that men could 'let themselves go' and still retain their attractiveness to women — well, as long as their wallets remained healthy. However, not to worry. This was just her imagination taking hold. Neither of them would get the chance at this alternate life. If Rachel had now replaced her as the preferred, newer model, she would have to pay the price. And if he now adored Rachel as he once did her, he would pay equally. And, at the same time, Gillian would hold on to him.

Her picture-perfect life might change, but the one thing not missing from the picture would be him. Yes, Vincent was, to the outside world, the perfect husband. He was undoubtedly good-looking, medium-tall with light brown hair, intelligent blue, blue eyes and an unassuming, boyish face. And then there was that endearing, slightly uncertain smile. He clearly adored her. He was intelligent, though she knew not quite as intelligent as she, he came from the best of families, had attended one of the more recognised universities and was an associate in a well-regarded law firm, was well heeled, and in public, attentive towards her. Yes, some aspects of this might be erased from within the frame, perhaps their social circle, for example. But she would still have the home, the money, all that she had become accustomed to, the Audi, the housekeeper, Chanel clothes, Louboutin shoes and expensive hairdressers. She would once again be the adored one. She would silently and anonymously cut him off at the knees, and then she would be his saviour. He would owe her everything.

"So, how was your day?" she asked. Cliché upon cliché. "Well, you know taxation law. Looking for loopholes in an ever-growing mountain of legislation. Who can keep on top of it? We try. But hey, I don't want to bore you with the details. What about you? All end OK?" Out of the mouths of taxation lawyers.

"Well, I managed to get bail for my latest small-time offender. Repeat offender, but that doesn't matter any more. He's not a flight risk and he's not a danger to the public, so tonight he's as free as you and I. Not the stuff I imagined when I went into criminal law. You know, high profile murder cases and all that. But that's only the television world it seems. Change of subject — Why don't I put some Ed Sheeran on and we forget about work for a while?"

They sat together quietly. Dinner could wait a little while. How, she contemplated, was she feeling right at this moment, with her world shattering before her eyes? Did she feel a sense of loss, terrible painful loss? Was her heart broken, as they say? She didn't really understand heartbreak. What she felt was simply a sense of unfairness that she had been usurped, and a need for vengeance. Did she love him? Did anyone actually love another person? Or did they love what that person brought to their life? She and Vincent had had thirteen years together. At this point, it seemed to her, they had it all. They had all the physical possessions. There was not only the loft in their sought-after part of the inner city, but the beach house, with ocean views, backing onto national park. They had an expensive but understated car. As well as all this, they were on all the guestlists to the best dinner parties, charity occasions and other gala events. Their photos appeared in the social pages of the city's publications. They mixed with other professionals and business successes. She supposed she did drink-up the attention. They themselves were a cliché, she realised. They belonged to an exclusive côterie. Vincent's social background - including attending the right school - had ensured them this enviable position. She, on her own, would never had achieved that. Oh, yes, as senior partner in her firm, she earned considerably more than he, though he earned well, but what he had brought to her life was status and social standing. Although, there *was* something else. He had loved her from the beginning. Without children there was *no one else but her.* And that was what she needed, what she had always craved.

She thought briefly about the increasing number of second

weddings they found themselves attending. The last one had been mid-forties stockbroker Jim Morgan marrying an early-thirties ex-model, who looked twenty. There seemed to be a superfluity of ex-models these days. Where and what had they modelled? She didn't seem to recognise any of them. What did a model become after her modelling life was over? Was their only option to snag themselves a specialist doctor, merchant banker or corporate lawyer to ease the way ahead? And were there enough of these men to go around? How many ex-models were there? And for how many years could the 'keto' or 'zone' diet or whatever the latest buzz was, the personal trainer and injections and laser, stave off the inevitable despoilment?

So much for intelligent men professing to be attracted to intelligent women. What really attracted them - him - was something more tangible and visible than that. It was youth and beauty. Particularly youth.

"Should we eat? I'll grill the fish." Vincent's voice returned her to the present. He smiled briefly, took himself back to the kitchen. "Change of plan. Let's eat in front of the television tonight," she replied. "I'll get the trays." While she would need to examine him for reactions, right now she did not feel in the mood for conversation, meeting each other's eyes across the dinner table. She needed time to compose herself for that. Tonight, her eyes might just betray her.

They watched BBC News and swapped routine comments on Brexit and the wins and losses in the tennis open.

Outside, a summer storm broke and heavy rain began falling quite suddenly, thunder rumbling. She got up, went to a window and drew the curtains. Lightning cracked across the distant sky. Not even the city lights could dim the brightness of its jagged assault. The weather seemed to be a metaphor for her own turmoil.

She would not, by choice, change a thing. But this was not about choices. There was never a choice when your rightful place was usurped by someone else, especially when that person was younger, more beautiful and above all, undeserving (but then again, what anyone deserves is in the eye of the beholder, isn't it?).

The alternative was inconceivable. She had earned her place in the scheme of things. Rachel had not. For her, it was all just falling into her lap, coming together too easily, just as it had all too easily for her little sister all those years ago.

She imagined a divorce, Vincent leaving her. She was familiar with the Family Court and the bitter proceedings, the losers, the crushed and humiliated.

Abandon all hope, ye who enter.

Vincent would stride out of there to the same life he had always led, and better. She imagined him in his picture-perfect life, though the picture would have changed. There would be a child's laughter, a gracious character house in the suburbs, which she suspected was what he secretly wanted, a backyard with a climbing tree and a swing and a barbecue grill. She herself would be alone. There would be no adoring partner putting her at the centre of his world. She thought of the property settlement, looked around her perfect loft with its lacquered black floors and monochromatic colour scheme. It would be sold and the money divided. What of the holiday house? What also of their social life where Rachel would take her place?

Of course, she would need further proof of his infidelity. But, if she was right, she would do something to bring Vincent back to her, and her only. Their future would be on her terms. Characters crossed the stage which was her life, and ultimately, exited. Life was a series of losses; she had come to know that. In the end, life's fluctuations signified nothing.

Just sound and fury.

VINCENT

I know I'm a bit of a bastard when it comes to the women. I'll give you that bro. Getting laid has never been much of a problem. Hell, I'm a law student. You know, that bit doesn't hurt. They're looking for a doctor, lawyer, Indian chief, not so? And I'll admit to the boyish good looks too.

Arrogant? Again, a little. Our law school review wasn't called 'Presumed Arrogant' for nothing. We were even a little proud of our reputation. Faint heart never won fair lady, as they say.

It's been like that for me with the chicks through four years of law school. But now, I don't know — now I've met Gillian and hell I'm a bit taken, I guess. She's something else.

I met her at yet another end-of-year celebration. Seems aeons ago now. It happened over the ubiquitous hummus dip and supermarket cheese platter, already tired and unappealing, only the broken crackers left. And there was just something, something about Gillian. The booze was BYO and cheap. Even if you could afford better, you wanted to fit in, not come off as the 'wealthy parents' prick (though quite a few of us were).

The flat was spartan. Near the windows, a few people smoked into the sultry December night. We might have been in a re-run of 'The Young Ones', with the sagging couch and the bicycle leaning against the bookshelves — a castoff from the parents — holding everything but books, the 'American

Psycho' poster on the wall (a bit recent for 'The Young Ones' but you get the picture). In ten short years, the residents and their guests would be installed in stylish apartments in upmarket suburbs and buying their furniture from Jardan or Coco Republic, eschewing Ikea and Freedom and others of those generic chains patronised by the masses.

She was dressed for the hot, sauna summer night in a thin cotton shift which skated over her perfect body, brushing it just barely in all the pertinent places. I felt the usual involuntary stirring in the groin. She was tallish but not too tall. Just right. And there you have Gillian summed up in a nutshell - just right.

I opened with an ironic, "Do you come here often?"

She smiled that instant, disarming smile that reached right to her eyes. I dropped my weapons. This was so comfortable.

"Well, not for the food."

"Want to come back to my place? I'm sure I can find something. Can't think what at the moment though."

"I wasn't thinking of a private dining room. Not on a first date. Is this a date?"

"I'm pleased you asked. OK, I'll go out with you. Could I maybe whisk you off then to something banal? Say, a charming little Italian that not many know about?"

That smile again. "How about a couple of pre-dinner drinks first? There's a deadly blue vodka mix over there in one of those glass dispensers."

We exchanged a couple of mandatory bits of personal life. She had just finished her third year of law at a different university, the one with the hallowed sandstone cloisters. So, I have me a clever one. There's something about scoring with a very intelligent woman. It makes the conquest that bit more satisfying, the triumph sweeter. And you don't have to work so hard. Some women turn reaching a climax into an Olympic sport — a bit slower on the turn, now speed up on the straight, keep going, keep going, don't stop.

We taxied to a curry place all students seem to know about. She didn't, thankfully, ask me my star-sign. Or what my favourite book is. A good start. She didn't pretend to just love football or pub-crawls with the boys. She didn't become earnest about the political scene or how the law treats women, no problems of the world to be solved. She was fun, relaxed. I haven't mentioned her superlative face, her lustrous, black hair falling in a perfect bob, her pale, grey-blue, disconcerting eyes unsettling my equilibrium, eyes that seemed to keep her at a distance, her soft skin that I just wanted to touch, her sculpted cheekbones and delicate jawline. Indescribable, though I've just tried.

She wanted to talk about my name, my namesake, *that* song. It *was* a starry night in this clear-skied, unpolluted Australian city. She teased me about the existential gloom in the song and laughed as I held my head in my hands despairingly and mimed a tableau of my mental suffering and torture. I parodied Van Gogh's loss of sanity. Me, who has not suffered a day of anguish or depression or even teenage angst in my short, privileged life. I assume it will always be thus. What do I know? She wanted to gaze, she said, a smile playing at the corners of her mouth, into my (Vincent's) eyes of cobalt blue.

Note to self — Find her a print of 'Starry Night' for her wall.

We finished the rest of a very good red.

We could walk home from here. I think she wanted to. By now, the temperature was more pleasant and a slight breeze disturbed the air. We strolled the old, bohemian, slightly down-at-heel, and yet expensive, streets of West End. The district boasts a mixed demographic — mostly young, well educated, Anglo-Celtic high earners as well as students, but still with a smattering of the early Greek citizens who had favoured the area a century and a half ago. Now the farms and much of the industrial activity — the gasworks, sawmills and joineries — were gone, the area gentrified. Some of the older men would be here tomorrow morning, drinking the traditional, strongly-brewed, black coffee over narratives of their lives.

We passed ethnic and organic grocery stores, restaurants of every variety, vegan a popular offering, and quirky cafes marked by their décor and ambience, as if entrenched firmly in the 70s. Dingy bars pulsated. Tomorrow, aspiring designers would be peddling their wares, alternative and vintage. We savoured the fusion of cultures and laughed as a sacred yoga chant emanated from one venue's open doorway.

At this time of night, the mostly young patrons have made a determined effort to appear part of a counter-culture, instantly recognisable to one another, even if more than adequately funded by conservative parents (who themselves had probably lived through the original hippie era of the 70s). Tie-dye, cheesecloth and hand-made sandals abounded.

We enjoyed it all but soon, away from the hub, were passing residential areas of stand-alone homes of historical character, weatherboard with verandas and tin roofing. Contrasting sharply were a few buildings of contemporary design. Urban renewal. Rising prices.

Out of the black, I thought about maybe having a keeper. I know. So un-me. A girlfriend? A partner? Significant other? What were you supposed to say these days? What was the acceptable term?

'I'd like you to meet my girlfriend.' High schooly, holdy-handsy, moony.

'My partner.' Sensible. Business-like. Mutually beneficial. Equal entitlement. All terms agreed upon. Did you need an ABN?

'My Significant Other.' Gender-neutral. Relationship status undisclosed, nobody's business. 'You may be accompanied to your appointment by a significant other.'

Until now, I could have been the author of 'The Subtle Art of Not Giving a Fuck.' Girls had come and gone. Nice chicks. Uncomplicated. Sometimes there was one I'd miss a bit. But never for long. Oh, I didn't treat them badly. I had been brought up to be courteous, polite, considerate. I had been raised a gentleman. It was just that, so far, I hadn't really cared. No girl had mattered that much. I could move on, have some more fun. I knew that one day, I would 'settle down', eat my peas and gravy, give all this away. It was what men in my circle did. Hell, I would be a lawyer, probably make partner (my parents had 'contacts', knew the right people.) Have a kid or two. A backyard. There were expectations.

Gillian would probably satisfy the olds. OK, she hadn't gone to the right private school and her parents weren't from their circle, but her selective school and university pedigree should more than compensate. She was smart. They'd have intelligent grandkids. And good-looking ones.

He had, at some time, flicked through one or two of those 'What a woman looks for in a man' self-improvement guides:

1. Respectful behaviour —

He shaped up there. He was well mannered, paid the bill, saw them home safely and so on.

Some women though, you had to admit, were not that easy to respect. Take those who looked for, made a career out of finding, and keeping, the perfect meal-ticket. Married, had kids, didn't ever again look for a real job that paid actual money. He saw them in the friends of his older brother. Oh, hubby may have set them up in their very own little boutique, which did not open 'til 10. She had such an eye for fashion, her best friends would say, after one of her expensive 'buying trips'. The boutique, in the best of suburbs, would be written up in exclusive magazines but never ran at a profit. In fact it was a liability while hubby worked 12-hour days to support it and her. At home, of course, she would redecorate to the accompaniment of 'oohs' and 'aahs' from her society friends. She had her own individual style, usually 'eclectic' which to her harassed husband usually meant a frigging mess, a balls-up. But he would never say so. She would never stoop to going along with a banal 'Scandi' or 'boho' (whatever the fuck that was) or the latest on-trend colour (sage, at the moment) in the populist, mass-produced 'home magazines'. She was just *so* creative.

And then there were those women (were they better or worse?) who 'lunched' and whose children were always 'gifted' and who volunteered at the (right school) tuckshop and kept the teacher under a microscope. If their children were not excelling, it was because they were not being 'challenged' enough or they were suffering from exam anxiety which would of course, require the best therapy.

A guy had to be very, very careful. And he would be.

2. Be genuinely interested in her —

(Are you excited to hear about her day when you get home?)

Dude, seriously? I mean, is there *any* guy, *anywhere*, who really wants to hear about a chick's day?

But hey, he could go through the motions. Not such a big ask.

3, 4 etc. They were a bit hazy. He knew he shaped up on the grooming, attractiveness, sense of humour kind of thing.

No problems really.

Was he really 'falling in love'? Hell, he was already contemplating what his parents would think, wasn't he? What was it he'd heard somewhere? Love was the only acceptable psychosis?

We walked under the jacaranda trees that the city was awash with, their translucent purple-blue blossoms a reminder that this was exam time of year. Beneath us, the ground was a floral, indigo carpet. We crossed the wide river, its still, dark waters hiding unimaginable, equally dark secrets.

A bit further and we reached her home. We kissed at the door. Not an overture but a prelude to some tender song that left me wanting more.

Throw your arms around me.

GILLIAN

Gillian had never wanted her parents' life. Even as a child she had known that, on some level. Children might often assume their parents' values but to her they had been suffocating.

Her parents had met at university where they were both studying the liberal arts. They had involved themselves in student politics, had shouted and carried placards and blocked the pathway of speakers whose views differed from theirs (their idea of a good time). They had seen the latter days of the Vietnam war and the enviable opportunity it provided to rail and condemn.

They had still been children during the much-vaunted social revolution of the 1960s (though they had, ironically, become the most conservative of parents). They still, however, favoured the music of those times — the 'Give Peace a Chance', 'Imagine', 'Blowin' in the Wind', 'Pave Paradise' genre.

Her mother, and father, were of course always vocal about the feminist movement. She thought of the dinner parties which rarely seemed to engender much fun.

'It's still women who take time off work to care for children.'

'People still frown upon them if they go back to work.'

'Mothers are made to feel guilty if they're not at home with their children.'

'And the criticism comes mainly from other women.'

And so on, and on, and on. Gillian puzzled over all that she heard.

Did anyone actually *want* these children?

The men always murmured their assent. Did they really think they had the better end of the stick?

Her parents had seemed to delight in misery. Any pleasure was perverse pleasure. She noticed the difference at the home of her friend Sylvie where there was happy chatter about holidays, outings, home renovations, food. She was drawn to this kind of household and loved sleepovers there, though she was too young to understand why the difference existed.

Her father had become a lecturer in modern history at university and her mother a secondary school English and history teacher. Their family had been comfortably well off, though they had lived in one of the more working-class suburbs as a matter of principle. Their friends were largely other academics. Their modest home remained largely in its original state. Her mother may have liked a new kitchen, but her father insisted that the one they had was perfectly functional, and that they, as a family, did not waste money on (bourgeois) things like that. He preferred to spend it on the type of holiday where the children would visit the sites symbolic of the country's revolutions such as the steps of Parliament House where the famous 'Dismissal' speech had taken place, the High Court where the Mabo decision ensured native title for the country's indigenous or the Ballarat site of the Eureka Stockade. Even her little sister was dragged along for a time, although too young to even remember. Perhaps her father had imagined that she would absorb the significance of the events through her pores. The family did not visit the famous national War Museum. They did not agree with war.

Gillian would learn as an adult that her family typified the kind labelled 'an enmeshed family'. Gillian looked back later on the photos of these holidays as lacking in any joy. They were lecture tours. She wanted a fashionable home, money and good times. She didn't care about making the world a better place. She cared about success and the trappings of success.

She knew that she would not be attending a private school. This made for more conversation with like-minded friends.

'It's time the government funding to non-government schools was cut off. The Teachers' Union has a policy of no government funding. If parents want to send their children, they should pay for it themselves.'

'They've got everything. Huge playing fields and sporting complexes, auditoriums, swimming pools, state-of-the art libraries. You name it.'

'All for the privileged, the elite. While so many public schools are disadvantaged and struggling.'

'Well, we won't be part of that. Gillian is doing so well; she shouldn't have any trouble getting into a selective school. And it will be co-ed as well. We want her to learn to mix with boys as her equal. Not find the right husband who she'll be second to all her life.'

In some ways, this tedious ambient noise served her well. It shaped her, but not in the manner her parents might have thought. Her aversion to its joylessness manifested in her choice of husband, career, home and lifestyle. Her father had dressed in corduroys, turtleneck and worn-looking, wool jacket. Her husband would wear a bespoke suit. Her mother wore a loose-fitting, cotton shirt and pants for the non-airconditioned government classroom. Gillian would dress in a tailored but feminine, designer suit. She would choose a well-paid and high-status job where she *would* probably meet the right husband. Friends would be successful, enjoy life and never be mind-numbingly political. In other words, she would live a life which was the antithesis of her parents'.

However, all this was secondary to the single largest influence on her and on the entirety of her life. When she was seven years old, her mother had become pregnant. Her parents had long ago given up on this, she had learned from overheard snippets of conversation. Her parents were always sensible to the point of farcical. This manifested itself here in the way they prepared her, Gillian, for the arrival of a sibling. Their carefully prepared monologues could have been taken verbatim from a textbook. They laid the groundwork first, reading her children's books about new siblings. They talked about her friends and their little brothers or sisters, following this with something like, "Someday, you may have a little brother or sister. Would you like that?" Gillian did not seem to be required to do any more than nod or say, "Yes." Her mother talked about how she felt when she was a child — "When my mother and father first brought my brother home, I wasn't too happy about it. But then I was happy to have someone to play with. And you're a big girl and you'll be able to be Mummy and Daddy's helper." When they actually broke the news, they sat Gillian down with them in the living room and told her that Mummy had a baby in her tummy and that the baby would arrive just before Christmas and that they would all mark the days off the calendar together every day. When asked how they felt about it, Gillian simply said, "Good." Job done.

The baby, another girl (isn't that wonderful?) duly arrived. Her parents sensibly included Gillian. She held the baby (Meg), pushed her in her pram on 'walkies', was told how helpful she was. Both her mother and father made sure they spent quality, individual time with Gillian, her 'special' time. In short, they did all the right things, as far as fell within their conscious control, but their unconscious actions were involuntary. Gillian noticed their rapt faces as they gazed adoringly down at Meg in her crib or their overjoyed smiles as she first smiled or, later, crawled. People in the street pronounced her 'such a pretty baby'. She grew to have golden, curly hair and green, brown-flecked eyes. She was happy, contented, an easy child — indeed the golden child — fussed over by all.

Gillian's value lay in her intelligence. Even at the age of seven she was recognised as 'intellectually gifted'. Her school reports were always exclaimed over. But she was never called pretty. Her hair was black and straight, her eyes grey-blue and almond-shaped. She was not to know that her particular, stunning beauty would bloom later. She also, as she was aware, although no-one else saw behind her façade, was not the easy, straightforward child that Meg was. While outwardly placid, her mind was busy, never still. She was already aware of that. When the teacher said, "Everybody get comfortable. You can sit in a beanbag if you like. Now close your eyes. Imagine yourself in your favourite place. Listen carefully to the sounds," Gillian was planning what she could accomplish after school (she hated to waste time), how she would make her essay the best in the class. And more recently, what could be done about Meg. Enchanting Meg. Exquisite Meg. Enraging Meg.

Frustration dogged her. Outwardly nothing could show. She was the good girl who always excelled, did the right thing, loved her little sister. Oh, little things would happen, just occasionally. Meg's favourite soft toy would inexplicably go missing. Gillian's school exercise book would be found with pages torn out, in Meg's bedroom; Gillian would protest, "Mummy, I'm sure Meg wouldn't do that," and put her arms protectively around her weeping sister.

Gillian tried harder than ever at school. This was her only weapon. Maybe she would prevail this way. But she observed impassionately the world around her. While her parents praised her, they clearly fussed around Meg. Gillian noticed also the effects of women's physical beauty in the world around her — on television, in film.

She came to see that she had been dethroned. Her rightful place had been usurped. She would have to find her own solution. It was the beginning of a dawning realisation that we are each alone in this world.

My life.

GILLIAN

Gillian did worry herself over Vincent wanting a child so badly. At times, she did consider giving him one. But the consequences to her were too great to contemplate. She knew that, no matter how much a couple loved each other, the love of a parent for their child was the deepest love of all, no matter how irrational that sometimes was. She had prepared meticulously for this eventuality. Planning and preparation were the key to everything in life. She was contemptuous of people who lurched from one juncture to another, each time having to mop up in the aftermath, wondering vaguely why things always went wrong. Crisis management. Life's victims. Gillian would never become a victim. It was simple really, something almost laughably trite that they had learned from the earliest days of workplace training — 'be proactive.'

Vincent's desire had been brought sharply into focus when they were invited to friends for lunch. Gillian watched their two little boys playing happily in the backyard where they had a barbecue. Vincent obviously delighted in chasing the gleefully squealing children around the disturbingly large grassed area. It had been worrying to see him so clearly captivated. However, her sense of his disappointment at her not having conceived had only been heightened. It was, though, the one thing she felt could not, would not, do to make their marriage perfect.

She had not wanted to go to the friends' get-together, but

she knew it was unwise to divulge that. The whole lunch in the backyard, Simon and Kim scenario, was abhorrent to her. Once upon a time, with Simon and Kim, evening get-togethers (not lunch-time to suit the kids and allow the bathtime — bedtime pitstop, in order to conform to routine and order) had been orgies of devil-may-care feasting and laughter and irony and liqueurs that continued through to the wee hours and reluctant 'a bientôts'. But now, Vincent, *barbecues?* What could be less intimate or cosily inviting, so not centred around her, than a barbecue! And the backyard! As far as Gillian was concerned, dining occurred inside and on gloriously mismatched but carefully selected chairs. Maybe not Vincent's first choice, but he indulged her. But not at a 'Barbecues Galore' 'outdoor setting' on bench seats and with paper napkins. Any laughter now seemed reserved for tales of the children's adorable little antics. Otherwise, conversation was, well, earnest. The cost of private schools, how they really should get their act together and enrol their sons soon. Any book their hosts had read seemed to be titled 'Raising Boys' or 'Self-Esteem for a Lifetime'.

And Vincent, acreage! Ride-on mowers. My God, in Macau they pack in two thousand one hundred people to every exhilarating square kilometre. This was all, she thought detachedly, so parochial. The house, it must be said, had everything. There was a media room, a playroom, a butler's pantry, three and a half bathrooms and a of course, a huge, paved, barbecue area. Just no soul.

The children were of course, they all chuckled, adorable. Adorable when the three-year-old interrupted the conversation with, "Ball, Daddy, play," or "Want drink, Mummy." Adorable when the thought you had was cut short by the toddler being consoled after a fall, or breast-fed (at the table, Vincent!) — nauseating, they had both always thought, once the *enfant terrible* was walking. Had they finished one single exchange today?

Once, she and Vincent would have Ubered home and then fallen in heaps, laughing about it all, taking turns to mock — 'Wow! Another half bathroom'. In recent times, however, his perspective had altered. He had become defensive of his friends who had pursued the kiddies/burbs dyadic bliss route. They were only doing what was best for the children, he said. What about what was best for the adults, she thought. Was parenthood just one long penance — sacrificing, one by one, all those indulgences and vanities that made your life worth living in the first place? And for what were you atoning? Was it all about the sins of the father after all? Generation upon generation? To Vincent, Simon and Kim had simply grown up. To have truly grown up it seemed you had to be yoked to a child or two.

Today then, there would be no shared cynical and flippant in-jokes. She did not want the sand to shift under her feet. Her coveted lifestyle depended on her being the ideal wife, who could change colour, chameleon-like, in order to survive. So, she bit her tongue. What a pleasant day they had had. What a lovely home, enchanting children. They must have them back. Such nice people.

Had Vincent breached some unspoken contract that bound them? On the surface, everything about the day had been perfect. The hosts had gone to so much trouble, but it had taken such an effort on her part to even get through it. She had just been unable to enjoy anything about it. She, Gillian, knew she should have their friends back but just couldn't muster the enthusiasm, however much she had once taken pleasure from their company.

To Vincent, she feigned dismay about her failure to conceive. She described her uncharacteristic loss of interest in her job and how she was having to put herself on automatic, fix a smile on her face and affect a cheerful demeanour to manage each day. Vincent comforted her, assured her that she was a very accomplished criminal lawyer who, he knew, assiduously kept abreast of changes to the Criminal Code and significant precedent cases. She was performing a vital role in a system where everyone was entitled to a defence. She did not ever tell him, tell anyone, that the satisfaction she took from the 'Not Guilty' verdicts she fought so hard for, was personal as well as professional. She viewed those who were charged with crimes as little more antisocial than the rest of humankind. People, in her experience, tended to overestimate their own virtue and rectitude. They were moral hypocrites when they tut-tutted over others' behaviour, broadcast in the media. Humans were, as she had experienced, wired to be vain, vengeful and selfish. For heaven's sake, our predilection for lying, vastly prevalent, begins at age two. Even babies can be manipulative in their crying. Our current affairs programs are predicated on our secret indulgence in schadenfreude. And just look at our propensity for sadism on social media where we are able to hide behind anonymity. As far as Gillian could see in the world around her, we did what we needed to do in order to survive. It was Darwinian really. Existentially necessary. The non-criminal amongst us were fortunate that stealing property had been denoted a crime, whereas stealing someone's husband or job had not. Abusing someone physically was a crime; abusing them emotionally was not. It was all arbitrary. The veil of civilisation only thinly concealed our basest natures. But to voice these beliefs would no doubt shock others in her profession.

Vincent was always supportive and reassuring.

"Honey, you have to stop beating yourself up. It's absolutely not true that you are letting me down. It's just one of those things. And anyway, there is every possibility that you will get pregnant. You mustn't lose hope. You're just used to succeeding at everything you do. You're a perfectionist. You work so hard and you get success. But this is different. Life is unpredictable. It can be cruel. [She in fact was under no illusion that life *was* predictable, or benign]. And look, there is every possibility that you *will* conceive. We just need to be patient. It'll just happen when it is meant to. I suppose being with Simon and Kim today didn't help."

"Well, it was a bit 'happy families'. But, apart from that, I *have* just had another birthday, and I don't know if I'm up for the rigours and disappointments of IVF. It all sounds so clinical."

"It does have a fair degree of success. And really, another birthday? Come on, you're young. Lots of women are having a child in their late thirties and early forties. Times have changed. Gillian, I hate seeing you this down. Promise me you'll stop worrying so much? We could look at adoption too. That's an option."

"I know. You're right. But I feel a bit as if I'm becoming isolated from family and friends. No-one else that we know has any experience of this. They can't possibly understand."

"Well, you've got me. And, when it's all said and done, I don't know about you, but I'm pretty happy being just the two of us anyway."

The problem was resolved, once again, for the time being. But for how long could she delay? Vincent had 'options' in mind. Would she have to go against her better sense and have a damned kid?

She thought of her favourite movie 'Gone with the Wind' and Rhett and Scarlett and Bonnie and the disaster wreaked by having a child.

A child always brought risk. Why risk the perfect life that they had established?

But a more immediate problem, now, was Rachel.

Rachel had to go, and it all came down to planning. Things only went wrong when people didn't plan, when they were stupid as so many people were.

Planning was always the secret of success.

She could never tolerate being second best, not to her sister, not in the workplace, and certainly not in her marriage.

It always came back to that. The primal fear. Rejection.

It had been thus since time immemorial.

Cain and Abel.

East of Eden.

VINCENT

He was having breakfast at a place on Eagle Street before going to work. He had told Gillian that he had to arrive early today, something about a deadline. How easily a lie slips off the tongue. But all it was about was that he wanted to be alone.

Morning commuters streamed by on their way to legal and stockbroking firms, even to the ASX. They all seemed oblivious to each other and already deep in thought. He observed the waiter, in his thirties and dressed in the obligatory black and white, tending to his up-market customers (who would each, Vincent thought, indulge their narcissism with involuntary, unformed feelings of superiority).

Hospitality staff always seemed to get the worst of it. Not only did they endure poor pay and unenviable hours, but were a medium through which others could assert their paltry authority — coffee too hot, too cold, lactose free, with almond milk, with coconut milk, turmeric, cake gluten-free, please; hot breakfast, but without the eschallots, with extra dukkah; eggs poached not fried. But the staff took it all without evident rancour.

(Did they really spit in your coffee or in the poaching eggs out the back?)

Nonetheless, he wondered if he envied the waiter just a little. He supposed he could put up with the vanities of the customers for the compensation of being free from the yoke of clients' problems, following him home every night and on weekends — working Friday nights and Saturdays. Alcohol seemed the only answer to that. He supposed that the waiter forgot his customers the minute he left the place. But then again, maybe he was wrong.

He contemplated a simpler life, like the guy in the Alice Cooper song 'You and Me' and his satisfaction with just a bed, his woman and the TV.

Could he really be happy without the benefits of social standing and money? Could Gillian? But then, these things had hardly been making him happy. He didn't really know what 'happiness' was, but he did know that what he had been feeling was unhappiness. He had a vague sense that he was acting out some preordained role. There had been certain expectations of him from the day he was born. Oh, he couldn't complain. He had been given the best of everything. He had been a bright enough, if not brilliant, student who had made his way into law with the help of very competent tutors. His father was a lawyer as was his brother. Barnwells became lawyers, didn't they? That was what they did. If he had studied psychology, he might have learned that they also, like Gillian's, would probably be categorised as an 'enmeshed family'. But it was all he had known. And how many men would have happily given their eye teeth to have what he had? Even his wife. The perfect wife, always agreeable, never one of those wives who has her husband dancing on strings, worried that he had stayed an hour too long at the pub after work and was now anxious about the reception he could expect when he got home. He saw so many of his mates in that situation with wives who expected eighty-hour weeks from their husbands, so that they could live their high income, high status lives. These friends of his gave the usual rueful farewells — 'Well, off home to the doghouse',

'Might be sleeping downstairs tonight', 'Wish me luck fellas', laughing but forlorn at the same time.

It seemed to him that they were victims of their own circumstances, snared in a trap of their own making. And yet they seemingly had it all — great job, attractive wife, beautiful children, a home in the right suburb. What was wrong with him that he felt they somehow had all been deceived? What else was there?

And he did not have that same suffocating wife at home. Gillian was wonderful. She was always happy to see him, always welcoming and uncomplaining. She didn't argue or sulk. Their sex life was good. So what was wrong with him? That was why he was sitting here in this café, alone, exploring his own mind, trying to identify just what it was that had him feeling this way and what he could do about it.

He knew that Gillian was central in some way to his emptiness. He felt that there was something within her that he just unable to reach, that though they were superficially compatible, they lacked some indefinable closeness. Her beautiful eyes were a wall that he could not get past. Gillian seemed quite content with the way they were, but he felt the need for a certain *je ne sais quoi*, that did not seem to be there.

Perhaps what was missing with Gillian was not sexual. Gillian was an imaginative, obliging lover. She was an expert in the mechanics of pleasure, as was he, a practised lover. Who wasn't these days? The nitty-gritty was explained everywhere you cared to look, in every magazine. She might have been squeamish about certain longings of his but, hey, you could pay for those and some of them occasionally did after a boys' night out at a strip club, explained away to their wives as some reunion or other. It was not her own pleasure that was missing either. She would often initiate an encounter. She liked to crouch over him and move in time to his driving deep inside her, into the abyss that proved at once so irresistible and so perilous.

No, it was not sensual deprivation that drove him to Rachel. It was a need more elusive, a need for connection that went deeper than the purely physical or compatible. Gillian was an attractive woman, and very much so. She was vain and careful to retain her slimness and tautness. In fact, he sensed that she had a fear of ageing as she checked herself in the mirror, turning this way and that, searching for any signs.

Yet of course, Rachel's lithe and pliant body, more than a decade younger than Gillian's, her silky skin, created a hunger in him that he could not deny. It now sustained him. He was addicted, had been from the first time he had walked her home on a drizzly evening. It had been a long day working together to prepare for a client's taxation audit. Had he imagined the glances between them, a slight coquettishness, her caprice now as he put his arm around her and drew her against himself to shelter under the umbrella? Did he imagine the current in the air? He wanted to ask her — Is there something going on between us? Am I crazy for thinking that?

They arrived at her city fringe studio apartment. Her home. She opened the door. He followed her in. The second she closed the door, he pulled her to him. Even in her high heels, she was petite compared to his willowy Gillian. He felt a power as he leaned down to kiss her, her face turned up to him. She hitched up her skirt as she ran her fingers over his aching groin. They moved to her bed. Afterwards, he knew that nothing could ever be the same.

It was more than her body and her youth. The sexual pull

between them was more than practised skill and mechanics. His desire now was for the very essence of her, her very centre, which she offered to him. She surrendered herself to him in a way that Gillian did not. Between him and Gillian was an indefinable schism. Rachel was complete abandon, a wantonness which thrilled him, and he was becoming hopelessly addicted to it. And afterwards, looking at her sweet face, he sank into her soft, molasses brown eyes and found peace and solace.

He did not think of leaving Gillian. They shared values of commitment, loyalty and mutual attentiveness. He had been raised by his parents to trust in these qualities. He could not even contemplate the consequences to his life and what it would do to his parents if he were to rip apart the life that he and Gillian shared. He had made every effort, since Rachel had become part of his life, to keep his life with Gillian normal. Their routine remained the same, their home was pleasant, they socialised as usual. Gillian could never know. She did not deserve the hurt. She had had her share of devastation as a child. The fault lay with him, not her. But he had to have Rachel. With Gillian, problems were never gone from his mind - work pressures, having a child, dissatisfactions. But with Rachel, all was forgotten. Sweet abandon.

Having his second coffee, he could think only in the present. If he tried to look ahead, everything blurred. Clinically, he knew that it would not be possible to live two lives forever. But beyond that, he could not think or act.

Quiet desperation.

There seemed to be no solution but to take each day as it came.

He left the café, walked a short way along Eagle Street

and took the lift to the eighth floor which his firm occupied. There were of course, lawyers already working. They always were, any night, any weekend. He sat at his solid oak desk and gazed out at the spectacular view of the wide, meandering Brisbane River. Yes, he had it all, almost anyway.

Soon Rachel would arrive, go to her small office next to his and then check in with him. He listened in anticipation, for the clicking of her heels on the polished floor, for that first glimpse of her. His need for her consumed him, her petite form, her slender legs, full breasts, caramel hair with the sheen of youth. The idea of Rachel was with him every moment. Another day was starting, a day which was a tantalising prelude to his next encounter with her. Periodically throughout his day, visions would come to him of her offering herself up to him, her areole a backdrop to her aroused nipples, his hand lightly caressing her arching back, inching slowly down, their hunger palpable. Could he get away early tonight?

Always on my mind.

GILLIAN

Rejection. She could not have articulated it as a child but that is what it all came down to. A powerful word with often shattering consequences.

Our recognition of its potency goes at least as far back as the time of Cain, that biblical figure whose offering was rejected by his father in favour of his brother Abel's. As we all know, Cain then slew Abel in a fit of jealousy and anger. Terrible consequences indeed. But this phenomenon by no means ended with these two brothers. Rejection has always, and always will be, one of life's most compelling motivators.

Rejection played a vital role in our evolutionary past where being ostracised was akin to a death sentence.

In contemporary society, the pain can be inflicted on others rather than on ourselves alone. We all have a fundamental need to belong and when we are rejected, the disconnection we feel is so agonising that it often creates surges of anger and aggression. Rejection has been demonstrated to lead to school shootings, violence against women and fired workers going on shooting sprees.

Rejection by a woman is a particular motive driving men to murder, even in as extreme a case as serial killer Ted Bundy, who admitted to taking the lives of at least thirty female college students before being sentenced to death, reportedly because he harboured a grudge against his first girlfriend who broke his heart. It is claimed that he even selected victims who closely resembled his former lover, Diane Edwards, an extremely attractive girl, pale-skinned and slim with long, dark hair and in the prime of her life.

Ted Bundy is far from alone.

What did all this have to do with Gillian?

Childhood rejection by a parent is not always overt nor intentional. It can be as an act of omission as surely as one of commission. For Gillian it came in the form of her younger sister Meg taking precedence over her seemingly without effort, simply because she was the pretty, uncomplicated one, the cherub. Gillian felt overlooked, ignored.

A little ray of sunshine.

From the day Meg was born, it seemed to Gillian, something she ached for, something almost indefinable, was withheld from her. While it appeared that Meg simply had to 'be', Gillian tried harder and harder to please. She tried harder than ever to excel at school. She lived for her parents' praise, their pride and approval when she brought home her school reports. Within her capabilities she helped at home as much as she could. She was always agreeable. Even as she began to develop her own opinions, she kept them to herself. She needed validation. And yet somehow, she knew that she did not inspire that same radiant glow in her parents' faces that Meg did. She found it hard to comprehend why her parents' friends, and other adults, always described her as 'placid', when inside all she felt was turmoil. But if she was wearing a mask, she knew that she had to keep wearing it.

Gradually, Gillian came to realise that she could only rely

on herself. There could be no compromise. She had to work things out for herself, make her own decisions, decide on what action needed to be taken.

Meg's fifth birthday duly arrived, in January. The fifth is always a special birthday and so it was for Meg. A party had been arranged. They were going to have it in a favourite park, a very pretty one adjoining the Brisbane River where they had on several occasions picnicked with their parents. It was in one of those better suburbs, as riverside suburbs generally were.

There were a large number of both adults and children as both friends and relatives had been invited. All the usual party games had been played, the birthday cake exclaimed at, the candles blown out, slices handed out on paper plates. Presents had been opened. The *coup de grace* was the one from Eve's parents. A Barbie doll. A doll that Gillian would later come to know was a rare Teresa version with golden hair and green, brown-flecked eyes. Just like Meg. How they must have searched for it, to please their adored child. How her parents rationalised this purchase in view of their much-vaunted gender equity stance, Gillian could not imagine. Even at her age she recognised the contradiction. Had she ever received such a special birthday present? She had only vague memories of her fifth birthday and could not remember her parents' gift on the occasion.

Gillian saw her chance. She had made her decision. She suggested a game of hide-and-seek, aware that her parents had run out of ways to keep all of the restless children amused. Her mother hesitated but then agreed.

"But no one is to go beyond the walking path. OK everyone? I'll say that again."

Meg was clutching her precious new doll.

The park was perfect for such a game. As in most old Brisbane parks, there were many large shady trees — jacarandas and camphor laurels. And for Gillian's purposes, there was the boat ramp. As a family, they had walked past the ramp on other occasions, even stopping to watch the water-skiers speeding across the water.

"Meg," she whispered, holding her sister's shoulders, "go straight to the boat ramp. I'll meet you there and show you the best hiding spot ever. We'll hide together."

Meg, ever the good child, just naturally good and obedient, whispered back, "But Mummy said not to go past the path."

Meg was also, however, easily persuaded by her adored big sister.

"It's OK, Meg. That's only for the little ones. I'll be with you so Mummy won't mind. Now quick. I'll see you in a few minutes."

Meg ran off. Between and under the many trees, little feet crunching through the pools of leaves which skirted them, Gillian ran off at a different angle. She would circle back to the boat ramp once she was out of sight. She saw the other children ducking behind trees and barbecues and rose gardens.

Within only a matter of minutes she had reached Meg. Fortunately, there were no cars or boats there. The ramp was not used much any more and any that had launched boats today, had left for the day some time earlier.

Gillian guided Meg, still clutching her doll to her, down to the end of the boat ramp to look for fish before they went and hid. What a great hidey-hole she had picked out for them! Meg would just love it. Gillian looked around. She could see no one. She shoved her sister, hard, from behind. She watched her flounder in the deep water, watched her struggle to stay afloat, to reach the ramp. She had just begun swimming lessons this summer. But it was to no avail. Meg was helpless against the river, swollen from the summer rains.

Her frantic, beseeching eyes met Gillian's. Gillian's eyes looked into Meg's impassively. She watched as her sister sank in the deep water, the current carrying her away. Gillian felt a strange lack of emotion, even relief. But it was done.

She took herself off by the route she had come and hid behind a tree where she was soon found. The children, all discovered, dribbled back from their hidey-holes. All were back except the birthday girl. They all waited. Then Meg's parents began calling her name. Gillian soon joined them. Before long, they all ran in different directions, still calling.

All in vain. No Meg.

Worry began to set in. Some children were crying, frightened. Gillian mimicked the appropriate emotions, something she had always been able to do, something she had learned. Parents were arriving to pick up their children. Panicked and confused voices spread the news. Some of the adults sprinted off on another frantic, fruitless search, commanded their upset offspring to stay put and not move.

At last, a call to the police was made, a terrifying admission that no one had wanted to make, a recognition that something really was wrong.

Police arrived, then more. Parents began taking their children home, shocked, fearful, knowing that it was now out of their hands. Finally, Gillian's mother took her home. Her father stayed behind.

At home, her mother was in a helpless state, something Gillian had never before witnessed. She sat in her armchair, her head in her hands, rocking backwards and forwards slightly. Gillian brought her a cup of tea which she clasped in both hands for comfort, and a sandwich, which just sat there untouched. Gillian heard her say quietly, "Please God, let her be safe. Please bring her home," praying to a God in whom she did not believe. The phone kept ringing, but they both ignored it.

Some hours later, Gillian's father arrived home. It was dark by then. He was in despair also. Gillian comforted them both. But she did not share their suffering, though they would never know that. She would soon have what she wanted, all their attention. It had not been so much that she was jealous of Meg, rather that, with Meg gone, she would once again gain what had originally been hers. And in the meanwhile, her parents' suffering would be the price they had to pay for dislodging her from centre stage.

Two police officers arrived. They wanted to inform the family as to the conduct of the search. A police helicopter would spend the night searching. Water police were already involved also. Local community members were also helping in a methodical search, dozens of people combing various areas, going out and buying batteries for torches. One officer asked for a recent photo, details of Meg's appearance and the clothes she was wearing for a Child Rescue Alert which was to be issued. The police were doing all they could.

Of course, looming large in the minds of everyone was the river. The mention of the Water Police made this possibility more real. Abduction also reared its head. Had they noticed anyone suspicious in the park? No, they hadn't. Was it like their daughter to wander? Again, no.

Unspoken was an accusation. How could responsible people like them, have allowed five-year-olds to have run off unaccompanied at all, much less in the vicinity of a river? While this question was not asked, Gillian's parents must have been torturing themselves with it, wondering how they had allowed this to happen.

This was to haunt them forever. Parents of the other children would later be talking together and levelling this charge. How could they have endangered their children as well as their own daughter? Gillian's parents were to lose friends and find people were distancing themselves from them. There would be no more dinner parties where they and their guests could indulge themselves in railing at the injustices of the world. None of that would matter any more.

To Gillian, this would mean that she would assume even more importance. Now her parents knew the pain of loss.

The news came at twelve noon. "We are terribly sorry to have to inform you…"

Even the slight hope her parents had clung to was now gone. For them, there was no turning back the clock, no fixing of mistakes, doing things differently. Their little ray of sunshine was forever gone from the world.

For Gillian it was all about planning for the future.

The Barbie Doll was never found.

Darkness at noon

HILARY

Gillian's night out with Hilary only reinforced her belief that you could not trust your life and future to a flawed system. You had to act yourself, and you had to act quickly. Otherwise, things slipped away from you, got out of hand.

So here she sat, having dinner and drinks in a favourite restaurant, Little Valley. It was to be another evening of listening to Hilary's pointless bitterness. She was recounting the weekend that should have alerted her to the beginnings of her husband's discontent. They had organised a house for a couple of nights in the mountains at beautiful Binna Burra, just a few hours easy driving from Brisbane. Her husband, Phil, had arranged the sojourn to support his good friend and work colleague, Cameron, who had separated from his wife and had a new woman in his life. It might be nice for Cameron if they were to extend the hand of friendship.

Phil was going straight from work with Cameron and picking up his new sweetheart. Gillian had learned that her name was Felicity. Phil had not met her yet. Hilary would leave work a little early so that she could collect the children from school and pick up some provisions for the weekend away.

With the children in the car, they were on the way. So far, so good. She had packed a bag for each of them the night before and made sandwiches to eat along the way. Drink bottles had been refilled before they left the school. There were books to read on the way. All seemed organised. Soon however came the plaint, "Mummy, I need to go to the toilet." So, Hilary pulled in at the next petrol station.

Next stop the shopping centre. She hadn't had time to make a list. She would just have to think on her feet. So, to the accompaniment of three voices saying, "Can we get this Mummy?" and her hastily made decision, "Yes", "No" — Hilary scooted round the shelves, mind racing through a checklist of food items. Steaks, sausages for the children, salad vegetables, cheeses, cold meats, eggs, on and on. Some treats for the children. Then, back to the car. Once again, they were on the way.

Some distance along, Oliver was carsick. Perhaps she should not have encouraged the children to read in the car. Another pitstop was needed until he felt better. This happened twice more, before finally, they reached the A-frame house. Miraculously, they were first there. Hilary was almost too worn out by now to appreciate the beauty and quiet of the rain forest setting. They carted all the bags from the car, unpacked the groceries, and changed from work clothes and school uniforms into jeans and T-shirts. Hilary had just enough time to touch up her makeup, brush her sensibly short hair and put together a quick salad, when they heard the first car pull up outside.

She didn't know precisely what she had expected, but it wasn't this.

Felicity could have stepped straight out of a magazine. She could not have been out of her twenties. Her high cheekbones, flawless pale skin and large melting eyes, lustrous dark hair swept back from her face, were reminiscent of a young Audrey Hepburn. She was perfectly slender and long-limbed, her fashion sense understated and elegant. Her nails were manicured and polished in an ecru gloss. Her makeup minimal, though subtly enhancing of her fine facial features. She looked fresh and ready for the evening.

Uptown girl.

Hilary recalled for Gillian how she had felt suddenly awkward and ungainly, aware of her little bit of extra weight, jeans and sneakers, clipped fingernails and tired makeup. For the first time in her life, the word 'matronly' came to mind. Trying not to appear flustered, she gave Felicity a beaming smile and said how pleased she was to meet her. Phil gave Hilary the customary peck on the cheek, ruffled the hair of his television-watching children, and then turned his attention to Cameron and Felicity. He insisted that they have the main bedroom with the en-suite bathroom. No, they mustn't protest, they were guests. Could Cameron manage the bags? What would they like to drink? Cameron had brought some wine that Felicity liked. They would all sit out on the large deck. It would be wonderful watching the pelting rain, listening to it pounding on the iron roof. Could Hilary put together a few nibbles?

Hilary at this point wanted to flop in front of the television, but of course, she would soldier on. She scratched together a platter of cheeses and antipasto, probably a little passé, but heck, what was she? Martha Stewart? Felicity, she noticed, did not touch the cheese or prosciutto, just a few olives and pickles. Watching her, as another woman, Hilary saw that she knew exactly how to use her lowered eyes, shy smile and soft voice to appeal to the men's protective and solicitous instincts. Hilary observed with incredulity.

Felicity was demure and self-effacing. Information about her had to be extracted bit by bit. Hilary would have been much happier had she fitted the bimbo mould. She and Phil could then have, later, shared their amusement with much mimicry and hilarity. But there was no pinning a bimbo tag on Felicity. The two of them oohed and aahed as Cameron revealed that she had just completed a Commerce degree and was now employed as an accountant in a city firm. How in the hell did she manage to look like that, after a gruelling day of solving taxation problems!

Hilary finally interrupted to ask if Phil could rustle up some sausages in bread rolls for the kids while she got them into their pyjamas. They could eat in front of the television. In the kitchen, Phil called out for her help. He could not, of course, find the bread rolls. He was enthusiastic about Felicity. Didn't she just have everything? Yes, it was so sad about Cameron's marriage, but he would still be supporting the children and had regular access to them. This kind of thing happened all the time, didn't it? Such was life. His wife might eventually have to move into something a bit smaller. And the children just loved Felicity, Cameron said. No harm done, really, Hilary thought a little bitterly.

Cameron's wife would be bound to start a new life for herself down the track, Phil said. She was, after all, still quite attractive. Hilary considered the words 'still' and 'quite' and their implications. And there were certain to be scads, queueing up asking for the hand of a woman in her early forties with two children still in secondary school.

She would have to snap out of this. It was nothing to do with her and Phil, none of their business. They had their own life, a full life and a happy one. What she was feeling was simply jealousy of this younger woman who, after all, had done nothing to hurt her.

Children attended to, more wine poured, Hilary asked her guests if they were happy to eat out on the deck. Such a cosy night sheltered from the rain. She apologised that dinner was just a steak and salad. Felicity looked uncomfortably at Cameron, who hesitated and then said, "Oh, I'm so sorry. Didn't Phil tell you that Felicity adheres to a strict vegan diet? No animal products. I'm sure I told him. He's just forgotten."

"I'm sure I told you, Hilary."

Felicity rushed in, obviously embarrassed. "It's quite OK, really. It won't be a problem. I'm perfectly happy to just have the salad."

Chastened, Hilary tried to fix things. "There's some smoked salmon there. Would you like that?" It was to have been for breakfast, but never mind.

"Oh, thanks so much, but it's no animal products. Not fish either."

Mumbled apologies all round. Phil had started cooking the steaks. Hilary brought him up to date, set the table, Felicity couldn't eat salad with feta cheese in it. Goat's milk. She couldn't just pick it out, there might still be a little animal product. Couldn't she just make herself another small bowl of salad? She didn't mind at all. The crusty bread too. Did Hilary still have the label? The wrapping was still on top of the kitchen tidy. It was fine. Thank God, no dairy product. What a relief that she could have berries for dessert, if not the apple crumble Hilary had bought from Jocelyn's Provisions.

The morning proved to be not much better. Felicity appeared, looking effortless in a pale blue, pure silk shirt — with jeans certainly, but edgy, not those like Hilary's with elastane for comfort. Her leather ankle boots were feminine and clearly Italian. Earrings were simple and genuine pearl. Cameron was certain there would be a vegan café in the village where he would take Felicity for breakfast. Phil vacillated. It would not be practicable to take the children. But would Hilary mind if he went? A vegan café would be a new experience for him. Yes, she most certainly would mind, but she really couldn't say so, could she, in front of everyone?

Breakfast over, she took the children on one of the shorter walks, the Rainforest Circuit. This was enough for her to throw off her unworthy thoughts and disconcerting feelings. Lamington National Park, was after all, some of the most beautiful mountain country anywhere. It would surely help her to put things back into perspective, for the moment anyway. The children happily navigated the winding pathway with its gentle slope, searching among the lush array of trees, ferns and vines, in varying shades of green, for the wildlife that lived there. They listened for the distinctive call of the bellbird. At the lookout, Hilary felt that they were surveying a new restful world, that they had, briefly, touched on a higher order of existence. Everything seemed clean and freshly washed. Sometime last night the rain had stopped, and sometime this morning, the sun had risen. The trees were sharply delineated, the sky a glaring blue as the Queensland sky is wont to be. How could anything be wrong, in a world so artfully arranged and presented in impossible hues?

Why then did she feel this unease, a sense that the sands were shifting? But there really was a change in the familiar landscape. Cameron and his wife, though the two wives were never close friends, were one of the constants in their lives. Were there really any fixtures that could be counted on? Hilary thought of Cameron's wife, her grief over the loss of what she had expected the rest of her life to be, her humiliation, her anger at her husband's betrayal. She thought of her resentment that he would do this now. Twenty years ago, there were men flirting with her, wanting her. But now, Cameron had had to go searching for the fountain of youth. For what? What would that bring him? Eternal lust? Another baby to adore for a brief time. And the new, young woman looked a good deal like his wife had back then. The same slender high-cheeked prettiness. So, was he just trying to relive his life?

Hilary recounted all this to Gillian, the events of the weekend, the beginnings of her self-doubt. Of course, both knew the outcome. Hilary's discomfort had been well-founded. Phil had been philandering, had finally relinquished his wife, home and children, his garden of Eden, for a taste of the forbidden fruit. Hilary returned to her current bitterness. She wanted to make the bastard pay. It was a pity we had introduced no-fault divorce.

Gillian commiserated, talked of the prospects for the property settlement, but angrily expressed to her friend that she thought it was the new woman who should pay most dearly. The usurper was most at fault. Gillian was not one to adhere for long to complicated interpretations of human intentions and blame. To her it was quite simple. She had not become a criminal lawyer by accident. If you stole, you paid a price proportionate to the value of the stolen property. All of Hilary's railings about whether you ever truly knew someone, about why and where to apportion blame were irrelevant. Of course, under the civil law, if you caused someone damage, well you paid compensation concomitant with the pain and suffering. Why should not that principle be applied to women who damaged other women's marriages?

Hilary seemed to Gillian to be impotent and unimaginative, only able to think of inflicting financial pain on Phil after her life had fallen apart. To her, that was simply flailing about, working within the confines of an inadequate legal system. Hilary, like most, had helplessly allowed events to unravel until it was all too late. She, Gillian, would impose her own justice as she had so many years ago. If the law would not help, she would help herself.

In the end, **she who dares, wins**.

RACHEL

Saturday morning, and Rachel sat in her small but stylish studio apartment, studying. In eighteen months, she would have finished her Law degree. She would enrol in a science degree as soon as she completed her practical training. Life ahead was full of promise. She knew with certainty the kind of life she would lead. Her GPA was high, and she would have her pick of law firms. But she wanted her career to begin with the prestigious partnership she was currently working for as a lowly paralegal on not quite $70,000 a year. Experience in corporate law would be valuable for the future that she wanted, and she would be able to move within the firm, into her chosen field later. Much of the work for Vincent was interesting enough, conducting research and helping him with case preparation, but she was too ambitious for that. She was bright and she wanted her rise to the top to happen quickly.

She aspired to specialise in patent law, her reason for wanting that science degree. The money was good, and the field highly regarded. The field of biotechnology was expanding all the time — genomics, immunology, pharmaceuticals, diagnostic testing. She felt excited thinking about it. All those fascinatingly bright expert witnesses. The fierce battle of giants. The huge amounts of money at stake. She would make partner in no time, but her ambitions ran higher than that.

Not for her, the prosecuting of sexual assault cases on a humble salary in the name of feminism. Women as eternal victims bored her. She did not have a chip on her shoulder when it came to men. She loved men. She loved their company and she loved good sex. She loved what they could do for her and was happy to use her considerable charms to achieve her ends, as women had always done. Hence Vincent.

She had met Vincent's wife at social occasions and, strangely, sensed in her, a kindred spirit. She could not understand though why Gillian had settled for him. Oh, he was charming and good-looking, had the right background, and was doing well enough. But he lacked a certain drive that she would have thought would be unattractive to someone like Gillian. The more Rachel got to know him, the more she felt that everything he had done had been out of others' expectations of him, not out of an inner ambition. He was beginning to bore her.

Gillian, she knew, had a brilliant legal mind and was a formidable criminal lawyer. Rachel would have imagined her with someone thirstier for success, on a trajectory to become a barrister and perhaps judge someday. She wondered just what it was that Gillian needed in a husband.

Rachel did want a husband one day. She had not yet met that person. What a couple they would make, both high profile in their careers. He would have a healthy wallet, allowing her to indulge her career as a barrister. She would be able to be selective as to which cases she would take, representing big pharmaceutical companies for example, even international clients. Certainly, as with her, her fantasy husband's self-esteem would derive from his own success rather than them pinning hopes on the future triumphs of some offspring. She did not want to sacrifice any of herself for children. She saw so many people do just that, live through their children, the high point of their lives being when their son made it into the first rugby team in their final year of school or their daughter gained entry into some therapy course or other at university. How many women had she seen who had compromised their careers in order to be 'better mothers'. Their alternative, of course, was to hand their infant over to a childcare centre or nanny, and Rachel did not think that was the right thing for a child's early years. She was a perfectionist. It was all or nothing. The concept of 'good enough' was foreign to her. If she were to have a child, she would want to give one hundred percent. But she wanted to have the perfect career. By definition, you could not give one hundred percent to both. She was not one of those who believed that a woman could 'have it all'. So, she had decided that motherhood was not for her. She had assumed that Gillian had not procreated for the same reason.

Rachel had watched her own mother, June, make that journey. She had, as had so many women of her generation, enrolled in and completed an arts degree on finishing secondary school. Her grades would have allowed her to do anything, but she had not received much encouragement. She anticipated also that she would marry and have children and it was all confusing. After completing her degree, she followed the path of many women and went into teaching. After all, as was so often pointed out, that would allow her to be at home after school and during school holidays for her future children.

This proved to be the case. June married and then Rachel's brother and Rachel duly arrived. Everything proceeded almost automatically as if to some pre-ordained plan. Their father,

Brian, continued faithfully to bring home the bacon in his public service job where he slowly but surely, moved upward through the ranks and pay scales, never rocking any boats. June returned to work in another government secondary school when the children reached pre-school.

She was not prepared however, for the ever-increasing workload, for the nights and weekends spent preparing and marking, and for the time taken from her family. She was not prepared for the steadily worsening behaviour, the hostility and disruption of the classrooms, bit by bit wearing her out and wearing her down. Fortunately, after a time, a new school principal allowed her to 'job share', so that she only worked three days a week. This, of course, put paid to any chance of promotion, though when she looked at what the people in promotional positions in state schools became, all that talking the talk, she knew that she did not want to be one of them.

Rachel and her brother grew up in a happy, gentle, stable home. Their life was pleasantly ordered and there were good times, fun times. Rachel loved and admired her mother greatly, even more so as she grew into a young adult and began to suspect what she may have sacrificed for her children, though her mother didn't ever say so. And her mother took such pleasure in her children, not only pride in their achievements, but from just simply having them in her life, that Rachel knew without any doubt that she experienced no regret or dissatisfaction. Nothing could ever have meant as much to her as they did.

In addition to their happy home, Rachel and her brother were given the best of education in the best private schools. Somehow her parents managed to pay for it all. They wanted to give their children all the opportunities they had not had, as did so many parents. There didn't seem to be even a bump in the road to their desired destination. Rachel accomplished the ranking to gain entry to law at the best university on leaving school, and had continued to excel.

As grateful as Rachel was to her mother, however, she did not want to be her mother. She did not want to be a mother at all. It would have to be left to her brother to provide the grandchildren she was sure her parents were looking forward to. To live in the cul-de-sac, have the barbecue in the backyard, the family car. Saturdays at school sport. He would love it all, she knew, but it was not for her.

As for Vincent, nice guy but maybe not the best catch she could aspire to. She was turning her attention to the senior partner, Howard, someone more in tune with her ambitious nature. She had begun to engage him, to hold his gaze for just a moment too long, a smile lingering about her lips, things that were instinctive to every woman. They seemed to know how to get what they wanted of men, even as children. Soon there would be an innocent invitation for a drink after work.

What was it that The Eagles had said about 'city girls finding out about opening doors with simply a smile'?

Where would this leave Vincent? Well, she would have to end it of course. She had no wish, none at all, to hurt Vincent but she could see no real problem there. He was certainly attached to Gillian. He could have never imagined that there was anything long-lasting in their affair. After all, that's what it was, an affair, by its nature temporary, ending as quickly as it had begun. She got around. That can't have been any secret. The time with Vincent had been sweet, for sure, but it had never been a forever thing. He could not, in all fairness, expect her to commit to something so obviously ephemeral. Even if he had nurtured thoughts of leaving Gillian, he was too complacent for Rachel as a serious prospect.

She would still have to work closely with him, of course, but they were both adults. It had been a fling, it was bound to end sometime, and it was over. He was a big boy. She couldn't see a problem. He wouldn't have to know she was seeing Howard if that was what eventuated. They would be able to look back and laugh, remembering.

Right at this moment though, she had to get back to her Saturday studying. She needed to maintain her high GPA. Her weeks followed in a pattern. Tuesdays and Thursdays were her university lecture nights. She would see Vincent one or two evenings when it was possible for him. She didn't ever cook, just ordered in. Friday afternoons she would shop in James Street, meet her only real friend Michelle, for a few drinks at Cru bar, or occasionally to eat at Gerard's. Saturday night was her alone time, which she cherished,

The weekends were strictly for studying, and maybe a family meal at her parent's home on Sunday evening. A cleaner came once a week.

Last night, she had met Michelle as per usual. Rachel was dressed in one of her angoras with a silk skirt from Alana Hill while Michelle wore a cute vintage favourite. She favoured op shop castoffs, something she tried to promote as a measure of helping to save the planet. Just occasionally, though, she couldn't resist something from Maiocchi.

"Rachel, you can find designer clothes in op shops," she told her friend once again. "I see silks and linens and other things all the time."

"They look great on you Mitch. You have that Annabel Crabb look — though younger of course — sort of a mix of intellectual with sweet and feminine. You were made for retro. But I would look all wrong. I just know it."

She didn't add that she really couldn't give a shit about the planet. She vaguely thought that climate change was probably happening, but there were people who would sort that out in the end. It was their job. Politicians, scientists and so on.

"I do recycle my rubbish, Mitch. I've even bought some eco-friendly cleaners for my cleaning lady."

"Great. Buying good quality clothes this way saves quite a bit of money though."

Rachel nodded in agreement. She thought to herself, that before long, she might have the senior partner buying her the odd designer outfit and item of jewellery. While she and Michelle told each other everything regarding their personal lives, she thought it a bit soon to mention Howard. It might not even happen. But the two young women had been friends forever, since childhood, and completely trusted each other not to gossip — or to judge, no matter how different their motivation or outlooks might be.

Michelle was the only person that Rachel had told about Vincent. Michelle had at first, been worried about her friend falling in love with him, but now knew that she had nothing to fret about there. She was not as sure as Rachel that he would accept the ending of their relationship as easily as she supposed, but if anyone could handle it, Rachel could.

They had chatted about the issues of the day. George Pell's conviction had just been upheld by two out of three judges of Victoria's Supreme Court. Many in the legal fraternity were unable to believe it, Rachel said. The standard of proof, 'beyond reasonable doubt', had not been met, they said. There was no hard evidence, no witness to what had allegedly occurred, no forensic evidence at all. Just one person's word against the other. Then there were the climate change protesters blocking traffic in the CBD. Michelle could understand where they were coming from but sounded a little dubious about the means. Rachel privately thought that they were just professional protesters who ought to get a job but didn't say so. She would not ever offend her friend. The topic turned to Michelle contemplating buying her first apartment, to locations and prices, to a contemporary who had just completed her Masters.

And so they chit-chatted. Rachel never felt as content as on these girls' evenings. Michelle was a treasure, a constant. She knew that Michelle felt the same, that it was a lifetime thing. Thick and thin. Not that they were expecting much of the thin.

You've got a friend

VINCENT

Vincent had arrived home from work early tonight.

"Gillian, could we sit down and talk for a few minutes? There is something I need your legal take on. Seriously."

They sat on the sofa, and she looked at her husband, her thoughts racing.

"It's to do with Howard, but it could involve the whole partnership. Our reputation, even its existence."

What are you talking about?"

"Howard came to my office for a talk today, Closed the door. He told me he has been involved in something that was bringing quite a lot of money in. It's probably all OK. He just wanted to be absolutely sure. You're a criminal lawyer so he wants me to ask you. We can't mention it to anyone else, of course. Not anyone."

"Well, get to it. What's he been doing? I can't believe I'm hearing this. Howard?"

"It's just that he may have been helping, facilitating — not doing it himself, just facilitating — the laundering of money for a foreign client. He didn't name him, of course. Howard suggested that he set up shell companies. He didn't say why, but I'm thinking it could only have been to hide the client's beneficial ownership. I mean, why else would he have done it?"

"Shit... Well, his advice to establish shell companies is not illegal in itself. He *is* a corporate lawyer, after all. It's a grey area really. A lawyer is not required to report beneficial ownership - professional independence, client confidentiality and all that - but they are required to be vigilant and ensure awareness of money laundering warning signs and risk management. But do you know whether Howard suspects he is dealing with the proceeds of crime? That's when he could be in real trouble.

"He hasn't said but he seems pretty nervous."

"It doesn't even have to be knowingly, just recklessly or negligently. Vincent, you really don't want him to reveal any more about it to you. Just in case. Just tell him I don't really know and leave it at that. Don't let him tell you any more about it."

"Christ. Proceeds of crime? I don't really think so. Can't imagine Howard."

"I know, but we don't always know people as well as we think. Even those close to us. Maybe you don't even know me as well as you think. Maybe I don't know you."

"Don't be ridiculous." He felt his face flush and averted his eyes.

"But really, if anything came of this it could, at the very least, harm the reputation of the partnership. All of us."

"It's extremely unlikely. Very careless of Howard though, to ask my advice without retaining me as a lawyer first. Then he would be protected by client confidentiality. I guess he knows that I wouldn't tell anyone. It might hurt you. But still."

Vincent's thoughts eventually turned to Rachel. She had been seeming a little distant, finding fewer nights for him. She had to study, she said. Was he losing her? And why? Maybe he was just imagining things. He would feel desolate if he were to lose her. Neither of them had ever talked of love. For him, it was adoration, something more than love. For her, he could not define what it was that he represented. She just seemed to be happy to be enfolded in my arms, cocooned, buffered against the world.

Physically, he hungered for her. And, it seemed, she for him. Their love making ranged from tenderness to a passion that was almost impossible to satisfy. Even in his earliest, most passionate days with Gillian, at the height of his need for her, he had never felt this rapture. Though they had loved each other, and still did in their symbiotic existence, lives where one would not function without the other, his life with Rachel was tangential to this, perhaps even in its own separate orbit.

Gillian had sensed his preoccupation.

"Vincent, let's be rash. You're home early. I haven't even started dinner. Let's eat out. Somewhere local."

Vincent was obviously somewhat subdued but he agreed, even tried to inject some enthusiasm.

"Sounds like a plan. How about Chow House? We could walk."

"It's a bit cold, I'd rather Uber."

They freshened up a bit and within half an hour, pulled up outside the restaurant. Gillian got out on her side and, as she turned to shut her door, glanced across the street. What she saw was something that caused her to take a short intake of breath. Even from the back it was unmistakably Howard and Rachel, he with his arm around her waist, disappearing through the sliding doors of the new, glamorous Calile Hotel.

Vincent carefully looking out for passing traffic, got out on his side and turned and walked to the footpath. They asked for a table for two and were seated and menus were proffered.

Vincent decided to order a draught Asahi beer, and after

some debate, a South Australian Heartland cab-sav. Waiting for the drinks to arrive, they each began to peruse the menu although they were already familiar with it. They checked with the waiter on the fish of the day. Spanish mackerel. They mulled over that for a bit but finally decided on the pork belly with scallops for him, beef cheek rendang for her.

Gillian was the one who now was preoccupied. She thought of Rachel and Howard and wondered about them. Had Rachel been sleeping with both Vincent and Howard at the same time? Or was Howard a new development and Vincent, maybe, on the way out? Had Vincent tired of Rachel? Perhaps she was saved. Perhaps she would not have to take action after all.

"How's the beef cheek?" Vincent broke into her thoughts.

"It's just great. Delicious. You know — I've had it here before, and loved it. I think it's my favourite curry of all time. Just falls apart, How's your pork?"

"Love it. Scallops beautifully seared. Pork belly crispy. Can't go past it."

Things between them had always been comfortable. Outwardly they still were. But both had only too sharp an awareness of a spectre of a third seat at the table. A spectre in their bed. To Gillian, this presence would definitely have to be swept from their lives. For Vincent, he felt desolate at the thought of losing Rachel.

If only he could get over her and go back to the perfect marriage they had had. While needing her and, he supposed, obsessed with her, there were times when he felt that he hated her and what she had done to his life. Maybe he should try a good therapist, find a way of understanding his feelings for her and then maybe disentangling himself, being again content without her. He supposed that his needs involved obsession or addiction which certainly indicated intervention by a professional. But he wasn't a therapy kind of guy. Going to a therapist meant weakness and shame.

The situation he was currently in, though, heaped guilt on his shoulders. He was carrying this weight every day and every night. It had become part of life. However, his desire to be free of it was outweighed by the pleasure of being with Rachel. Sitting here with Gillian now, he was wracked with it. If only he could confess his affair to her, unburden himself. He was so tired of the lying. That, though, was impossible.

They both tried to make the evening pleasant, but it did not sparkle as it would once have. Both were preoccupied. Something had to happen. They could not go on like this. At least, Gillian had thought, once Vincent knew about Howard, he would see Rachel for what she was. Perhaps he would sack her, although that would be awkward to explain to the partners, to Howard, and she may involve Fair Work Australia. Or maybe it was the other way around, that Vincent had tired of Rachel. Perhaps they would both be able to accept it for what it was, an office romance that was over, and move on like two adults.

"What do you think about taking a week or two off, go up to Noosa for a break? We could probably do with it. It's nice up there at this time of the year and the school holidays are weeks away so it should be quiet. I could get away from work at the moment without too much of a problem." This from Gillian.

"Sorry, hon, a bit hard for me to just drop everything right now at a moment's notice. Too much going on. Not very fair to the others. Maybe more towards the end of the year, before the Christmas school holidays."

"OK, it was just a thought. A pleasant thought. But if you can't, you can't. We could do a weekend or two though. Leave on Friday night after the traffic. Try to start back before the traffic on Sunday."

Dinner finished, plates whisked away, a 'no' to the waiter's enquiry about desserts or coffee, Vincent turned the conversation back to lawyers and money laundering, obviously something that was niggling at him.

"Vin, look," Gillian responded. "Shell companies are generally created for legitimate commercial reasons. You know that. The average corporate lawyer has probably set up a number of them. Lawyers in Australia are probably unintentionally caught up in money laundering schemes when foreign investors use the property market for this sort of thing. The main thing they can do if they're worried, is to screen their clients, get as much personal information from them as they can. It's often very difficult to find out the source of their funds. But that's not what's happening here. And whatever it is that Howard has got himself into, he can't discuss the client with you. Probably shouldn't have said as much as he has. So, you're in the clear."

"It could involve the firm's reputation though, if anything ever got out. And what about the proceeds of crime thing though?"

"Look, I'm sure that Howard would have been prudent and screened the client. And in this country, a lawyer is not required to report information on ownership. I really think you're worrying about nothing. What say we have the partners from corporate over for dinner sometime soon? We haven't done that for ages. Being in a social situation with Howard may put things into perspective."

What a support, a wife, a friend, Gillian always was. He was so very lucky to have her.

The last of the wine having been drunk, the bill paid, a few minutes wait for another Uber and they were heading home. To where he had everything he could ever want. He was sure it was only a matter of time before that included a child.

All at risk because of succumbing to the temptations of another woman.

Original sin — the forbidden fruit.

GILLIAN

First to arrive were Adrian McConnaghey and his wife Cynthia. Adrian was in his late forties and looked the part of corporate lawyer, slim and straight-backed with a preference for Italian shoes polished in accordance with religious zeal — as if footwear were the measure of the man — silk socks and expensive suits. His hair was turning silver and his face lean and haughty, framing eyes of steel blue. Even tonight, for an at-home dinner, he had not relaxed his standards.

Cynthia was dressed in ice blue silk — Alannah Hill, Gillian guessed — and pale, matching, floral-print heels. Her straight, mid-brown hair fell perfectly to sit just on her shoulders. She was, as always, overly cheerful in contrast to her husband's reserve, as if to compensate for some deficiency. Did this stem, Gillian has at times wondered, from Adrian's occasional attempt at humour as he sledged his wife's soft Arts degree education and forays into the fields of linguistics and French language, ventures which he viewed with barely concealed disdain? Cynthia had at times toyed with the idea of returning to secondary teaching, but Adrian had shown little enthusiasm, concerned that this might interfere with the smooth running of the household, and in any case, paid a pittance. What was the point? And how did she think she would manage smartboards and e-marking? Things had changed since she had been in the workforce. Besides, she would soon have a grandchild to keep her busy.

Adrian was holding forth on something to do with some corporate restructuring he was involved in, as Vincent offered him a wine. Oh, could Vincent get the glasses from the buffet please? Gillian had neglected to do so. Gillian guided Cynthia to the bedroom to deposit her handbag and catch up on how the children were doing — and was she still enjoying book club and U3A?

The next guests arrived — Alex Haynes and his wife Deborah. Only in his early forties, his amicable manner belied his formidable intelligence and the complex legal world he inhabited. Always reluctant to talk work at social occasions, he was like everybody's favourite uncle (though somewhat younger) and could be mistaken for the man who ran the local fruit and veg shop. Tonight, he wore his usual sunny smile which reached his warm brown eyes, his geniality accentuated by his full cheeks and smooth crown. He was dressed in fawn slacks, a cream Brooks Brothers shirt and brown leather loafers. After giving Gillian a peck on the cheek, and telling Vincent what a lucky man he is, he managed to turn the conversation to rugby and what a mess it was in.

Deborah commented on the beautiful apartment, effusing over how wonderful it must be to live here but that they were tied to a house in the burbs, at least until their children had grown and left the nest. She was dressed simply in an ivory linen shift and tan pumps. She presented Gillian with a bunch of proteas and turned to engage in conversation with Cynthia, lamenting that they didn't catch up often enough. Gillian arranged the flowers in a vase, thinking how obvious it was that Alex and Deborah had a happy marriage, how they never bickered after a few drinks, stroked each other's arms almost unconsciously. But then she and Vincent were close too, still loved each other. Would Alex Haynes have become sexually involved with his para?

Good vibrations.

Belinda Braithwaite was the only female partner of the corporate group. Her qualifications and specialist knowledge were impressive. She was poised and confident, late thirties, pretty and trim. Her long, butterscotch hair was tonight tied back, and she was wearing a form-fitting, midnight-blue sheath and Dorothy-red stilettos embellished with crystals. Her earrings were sapphire, her hands unadorned. She could as easily have worked in fashion as she did in trademarks and the development of brands. Her elusive partner was absent tonight, as he so often was from work occasions. Gillian knew that Belinda and Brad lived separately, that he was a property developer. Belinda was always pleasant but private, her personal life kept firmly in the background.

It befitted Howard Brookes to arrive last, with his wife Ann. His was a presence that bespoke his innate authority. The senior member of the group, he commanded a respect borne of vast achievement and fierce loyalty to the partners. He is a man of moral purpose and professional dedication. Gillian wondered at his apparent liaison with Rachel. Did we ever truly know anyone? Howard had always been a big man but was beginning to put on a little more weight and his features were thickening. He had a grimness of expression which was at odds with his essential kindness and sense of humour. He was wearing a dark navy suit, tailored to fit his increasing bulk. His infidelity, Gillian thought, did not sit easily. And it would undoubtedly have consequences. What was he contemplating?

The loss of his marriage? Of self-respect, or the respect of others? What was life, though, if not a series of losses?

Ann, in contrast to Howard, was rather colourless, or so people saw her. It was difficult to get to know her. Perhaps there was more to her than met the eye. She was small and very thin, with short, light brown hair and mid-blue eyes that darted about uncertainly. She seemed to stand in Howard's shadow, always agreeable, aiming to please. She was a bookkeeper in earlier life. Now she 'does volunteer work' on other specific, set-in-stone days of the week. She was dressed tonight in a cream, silk shirt with pussy bow, tartan, pleated skirt and brown lace-ups. She never seemed to get it right.

Gillian had been ushering them all into the living room with its plush mint sofa and emerald green velvet armchairs, paintings large and abstract. Vincent made sure his guests' wineglasses were filled and Gillian offered appetisers of scallops and smoked salmon.

There was the usual, to be expected, chitchat around how people's families were keeping, what people were doing for Christmas, whether anyone was people planning a holiday or trip. Add the ubiquitous comment on the news of the day — the never-ending drought, the bushfires, the disastrous Prince Andrew interview — but, thankfully, never politics, never Chinese land acquisition, property prices or any other topic already done to death by the media, even social media.

Gillian and Vincent moved to the kitchen where she put finishing touches to the home-made gnocchi with smoked ricotta and pumpkin, and Vincent added fresh wineglasses to the table setting and invited the guests to sit. They had decided on Australian wines only, and for the first course, offered a choice of Riesling, rose or pinot grigio.

Conversation turned to this and that. Of course, there was horror at the deaths of two children, aged one and two, who had been left in the family car by their mother for a period of up to seven hours. The mother had been charged with two counts of murder along with drug offences, was being held in remand and faced a lengthy term in prison. The community at large, seemed for the most part, to be baying for the twenty-seven-year-old single mother's blood, if you could believe all that you read.

Adrian kickstarted the conversation.

"Gillian, you're the criminal lawyer. How is it that the mother has been charged with murder? She couldn't have intended to kill her children. Gnocchi's great by the way. Perfect."

"Thank you, Adrian. You can come again. Well, for one thing, the definition of 'murder' in the Queensland Criminal Code was expanded earlier this year, in March. It now includes 'an act or omission done with reckless indifference to human life'. So, this is an alternative to intent."

"That's a big one. 'Intent' seems reasonably clear. But 'reckless indifference' is fairly subjective, don't you think? I wonder how prosecutors are going to deal with that," said Cynthia.

"Yes, it's going to be interesting. And this is the first case in Queensland to be prosecuted under the new provision. They have had these grounds for murder in New South Wales for a while now. But they haven't had a case like this. And yes, it is absolutely a subjective test. The jury will be asked to decide whether the *defendant* foresaw the probability of her actions resulting in death. Not 'a reasonable person'. And not just the *possibility*."

Deborah replied, "And people seem to want to see this woman drawn and quartered. Seems to me she's been punished enough."

"Yes, the Law Society president is asking whether we really want to see her punished to the same extent as a hired hitman," said Howard.

Alex brought the seriousness to an end with a lighter comment. "Well, I suppose none of us here knows which one of us will be the next murderer under this reckless indifference stuff. Better not drink too much tonight." There was a little laughter.

"If anyone here is the type, it's you Alex," countered Vincent, a comment that may in hindsight be seen as ironic.

"Actually, I'm not sure there is a type," Belinda chipped in. "Most of the inmates in Sir David Longlands didn't know they were a murderer until they killed someone."

Gillian and Vincent gathered plates and checked on the main course, glazed salmon with ponzu. Gillian served and Vincent refreshed wines, replacing glasses where needed.

There was general enthusiasm, once again, for the food and wine.

"I don't know how you do it, Gillian — and Vincent — after working in such demanding jobs,' said Deborah.

"We aren't bringing up children yet," Gillian replied. "Yours haven't even reached their teens yet, have they? That's what I see as hard work."

"No, Sarah starts high school next year and Michelle in two years' time. We know how stressful the high school years can be, on the whole family. But we do have a housekeeper. Couldn't manage without her."

"See Adrian, we could do it. I could go back to work. If

we had enough help in the house," Cynthia said.

"Damned if I know why women are always so keen to be in the workforce, especially when they don't have to be," answered Adrian. "I wouldn't mind staying at home, organising a cleaner, a bit of shopping, cooking."

"Careful, you're on dangerous ground there, mate," said Vincent, laughing. 'You don't want to have to call on Deborah for legal advice."

"No, you're right there," Deborah agreed. "We see the outcome of divorce every day, bitterness over custody and property division. I think maybe the good old days had something going for them, when people held the family together, through thick and thin. Before 'no fault divorce' arrived, in 1975."

"Yes, all that business of private investigators sneaking around with cameras, taking photos of adulterous husbands in bed with their paramours. And heaven help you if you were the guilty party in a divorce. You certainly got punished in the property settlement. Better to behave yourself back then," Alex chimed in.

"Now men can just walk out on their wives for the younger woman, there's no public shaming, no punitive settlement," said Ann, usually reluctant to wade in on contentious matters. Gillian couldn't help but wonder if she knew about Howard and Rachel.

"It's a wonder there aren't more murders," Belinda responded.

More chit chat. Dessert arrived. Coffees. Goodbyes and thankyous. Guests departed. Clean up began.

With Vincent in the bathroom, Gillian, using a cloth, carefully picked up Howard's wineglass by the base, wiped the lip well, and popped it into a sealable bag and then into a handbag in her wardrobe. She had, just yesterday, bought seven more of those wineglasses at Wheel and Barrow.

The best laid plans...

VINCENT

Rachel Klein was dead. It had happened only the night before last, a Wednesday. Vincent had been surprised when she had not phoned in on Thursday morning, and had rung her without success. Her cleaner had found her that very morning, had come running out of the building, horrified, and then rung the police, hardly making sense. But then all they needed was the word 'dead' and an address.

In the office, everyone was in shock, some asking pointless questions, offering pointless opinions, some remaining silent. 'How?', 'Who?', 'Someone on ice probably.' One theme emerged. It had to be a stranger. Everybody liked her. No one could think of any reason to kill her. What did Vincent think? He was the one who saw her the most, who worked so closely with her.

Vincent, while as unbelieving as everyone else, tried to recognise the feelings within himself. Shock, of course. He was asking himself the same questions that had been left hanging in the air of the office, almost tangible as if waiting for others. He was bewildered, but he did not feel a sense of desolation, as he had ever since she had told him that it was over, that there was someone else. She would not tell him who. He had not been able to let go. He could share her, he said. He had been prepared to accept any crumbs she would drop for him. He had no pride. He despised himself but could do nothing about it. He kept ringing her phone, even after she had stopped answering. He hovered outside her apartment building, even twice buzzing her intercom, only to be told that no, he couldn't come in. At work, relations were polite but strained. She had asked him to please stop calling her.

All that was over now, now that she was dead.

What he did feel though, he had to admit to himself, was a sense of satisfaction that Rachel had got what she deserved. And for that, he felt neither shame nor guilt. Someone had done what he, in his imagination, would have liked to have done.

Howard took charge at the office. No one, he said, was to go into Rachel's office, in anticipation of a visit by police. They would almost certainly all be questioned. He asked them to give some thought as to whether there was anything, no matter how small it may seem, that they could tell the police about Rachel's life or the people she knew. They owed at least that to her. To help the police find her killer.

The appearance of the police came surprisingly early in the day. Vincent, of course, was interviewed along with everyone else.

"Mr Barnwell? Vincent Barnwell? Detectives Copeland and Morrison. Could we have a few moments of your time? Just some routine enquiries."

"Of course. Please have a seat. How can I help?"

"I'm sure you've heard the news about Rachel Klein."

"Yes. It's unbelievable. We're all still in shock here. This is not something you ever expect. Not in your own backyard anyway. What happened? How was she killed? Was it a break in?"

"I'm afraid we're not at liberty to disclose any of that just yet, sir. You worked closely with her, I gather?"

"Yes, she's my — well, was my paralegal. She helped with research, drafting legal documents, business documents, that sort of thing. So yes, we had to work closely much of the time"

"Did you do all the work together here in the office, Mr Barnwell? Did you ever have occasion to work together at home, after hours say?"

Vincent's mind was racing. Of course, he imagined, his fingerprints would be all over Rachel's apartment which of course they would search. There was no point in saying no. Who had ever anticipated this?

"There have been a few times, not often."

"At Ms Klein's home, or yours?"

"It was at her place. Only a few times, as I have said."

"And when would be the most recent occurrence, sir?"

Vincent's stomach began to churn. He tugged at his collar.

"Umm, it has been a couple of months." (He knew to the day when the last time he had been.) I couldn't say exactly."

They suddenly changed tack.

"Has she mentioned anyone who might wish to harm her? Any social media threats?"

"Absolutely not. I can't imagine anyone who would want to hurt Rachel. I don't know much about her university life. She didn't really talk about it at any great length. Her lectures were at night, so probably not a lot of socialising was going on."

"Had her mood altered lately? Did she appear worried or preoccupied, in your estimation?"

"Nothing that I've noticed, Detective."

"Well, that will be all. Sorry to have taken up your time. Just routine enquiries as we said. Thank you for your cooperation. Oh, we will have to send for her computer sometime today. Please don't log on to it at all.'"

The detectives stood and Vincent hastened round the desk to open the office door but they were already leaving.

They proceeded to 'have a few minutes' of the time of all the other of the firm's employees, while Vincent tried to compose himself. He did not know why he was feeling such discomfort. He was totally innocent. He had nothing to worry about. But not telling the police everything, leaving out their affair, was making him extremely uncomfortable. He had no experience in dealing with the police but this omission, he knew, was not right.

Why had he not told them? He supposed he did not want any spotlight falling on him. It was just an instinct that you followed, some base self-protective reaction.

He wondered what the police were hearing from the other staff. Did anyone have any inkling that he and Rachel had been seeing each other? The had believed that they were concealing their little secret very well.

He called Gillian. She had not accessed the media at all, not heard the brief reports of 'a young woman found dead in her Teneriffe apartment, police still confirming her identity. Her death is being treated as suspicious'. Gillian's reaction was predictable. No. She could not believe it. Who could have done such a thing? And why? What had the police said? And how was he, Vincent, holding up? She would leave work and join him if he wanted to spend the rest of the day at home. But the last thing he wanted was Gillian's solicitousness, conversing with her about Rachel.

The police would, right now, be trawling through Rachel's home, now a crime scene, lifting fingerprints, vacuuming for fibres, analysing blood splatter. Talking to neighbours. There was no CCTV at her small apartment block, no onsite managers to talk to about comings and goings. Everyone knew about DNA, but Vincent was unsure of the specifics of collecting it. Rachel's parents would be identifying the body. Cause of death would be determined. None of this seemed real.

The detectives finished their interviewing and departed. Howard called the staff together again. He thanked them all for being so co-operative and asked them all to respect the privacy of Rachel and her family and to please not talk to the media at all. They would possibly be hounded by a press, hungry for juicy details. He would be visiting Rachel's parents and would convey condolences.

It was not to be long before her identify was released on television news and in the print media. Cause of death was also released. Rachel Klein had been 'brutally bludgeoned' to death in her home. Police were conducting enquiries. Would anyone who could provide any information please come forward?

The press, of course, were in their usual feeding frenzy. A bright, beautiful girl, elite private school graduate, studying Law, now deceased. Vincent could not help but wonder if the reporting of her murder would have occupied so much space, day after day, if she had been a supermarket checkout operator from the wrong school, wrong suburb, generally the wrong side of the tracks.

Linda Bishop
LAW STUDENT FOUND BRUTALLY MURDERED
A woman has been murdered in a vicious bashing attack in Brisbane.

The 26-year-old was killed at an apartment in the inner

suburb of Teneriffe on Wednesday, 10th October.

Rachel Klein, a former student of an elite private girls' school, was employed as a paralegal at a Brisbane law firm and was studying Law at the University of Queensland. Her family have released a statement through Queensland Police requesting privacy.

'While her family appreciate the support offered by the community, they have requested their privacy at this difficult time,' the statement read.

Klein's mother told nine news that her daughter was 'a beautiful, loving, young woman who had studied hard and had a bright future ahead of her.'

Friend Michelle Harmer said that she had known Klein since their early school days and told Guardian Australia she was 'an incredible person in every way.'

"She was a loyal friend," she said. "I cannot describe how heartbroken I am at this moment."

Outside her building on Thursday, Klein's neighbour Greta Davey, told Guardian Australia that she was home at the time of the alleged murder but that the first she heard about the attack was on the news.

"I didn't hear anything," she said. "I was at home watching the news about the attack and then saw it was our building."

Howard Brookes, senior partner at the law firm where Klein was working, said that this was a terrible tragedy. He said that this violence against women had to stop.

Klein's death has horrified Brisbane.

Vincent was beginning to feel a sense of panic. Would his affair with Rachel become known? What about Michelle?

Would Rachel have confided in her? Surely not, he tried to calm himself. But what if she had? Would the police interview her? He wondered who the new man in Rachel's life was and if she had told him about Vincent. But surely the police would not know about him, would not be speaking to him. He felt panicked at the thought of Gillian ever finding out. But he was not a suspect. He had nothing to do with Rachel's death. Even if the police came to know about the affair, there would be no reason for them to divulge it to Gillian.

Calm down, he told himself. You're worrying about nothing. However, there it was, still niggling at him in spite of his rationalisation.

Oh! what a tangled web we weave.

MICHELLE

Michelle opened the door to two detectives.

"Ms Hildebrande? Detectives Copeland and Morrison. Could we have a few moments of your time in connection with the death of Rachel Klein?"

"Please, come in."

Shown into the living room, the detectives took in the ambience that Michelle had created for her sanctuary from the world. Whereas Rachel's apartment had exuded some notion of the 'Scandi' that had been so much favoured in recent years (Detective Morrison hadn't been able to escape 'The Block', his wife being addicted to it), Michelle's exhibited what he vaguely recognised as 'boho'. Rachel had styled her abode sparingly, using soft pinks and blues and blonde timber, a touch of grey. Michelle's place, on the other hand, was quite a jumble of variously coloured cushions and throws, hand-crafted pieces of art on the walls and adorning mismatched coffee and side tables. Women, the detective thought.

Michelle was aware of her appearance. She was still dressed at 10 a.m. on a Friday, in the T-shirt and trackpants she had slept in. She was still trying to absorb the fact that Rachel was dead. Things like this just didn't happen in her world. And who? Who could possibly have done it? The people in Rachel's life were just not murderers. But if anyone knew Rachel, really knew her, it was Michelle, and she was certainly aware that where men were concerned, she had a bit of a wild side. Had she picked up some successful looking man in a bar and then taken him home? Had some ice addict broken into her home?

"Sit down, please," she said.

Even as unable to focus as she was, she did think to offer them tea or coffee. Both thanked her and opted for coffee.

Coffee made, Michelle seated, the questions began.

"We gather that you were a close friend of Rachel Klein's, Ms Hildebrande?"

"Yes, we have been friends since school. I consider myself to be her closest friend. We spend pretty much every Friday night together. We keep that night for each other." She was unaware that she was still speaking in the present tense. "But how did this happen? Did someone break in? How was she killed? Do you have any idea who might have done this? I mean, I still can't believe it. I just can't believe it."

"Ms Hildebrande, I'm sorry. We realise how hard this must be for you, but I'm afraid we are not at liberty to reveal any of the details at this stage. We can tell you that we have not taken anyone into custody in connection with any of this."

There were things that they knew, of course. There was no sign of a break-in. No one had even tried to stage a break-in. The perpetrator had either let themselves in, or been let in, presumably by Rachel. In almost half of murder cases, the victim and the killer know each other well. The motivation was often a broken love affair, a marriage gone sour, jealousy.

They knew that Rachel had been killed from behind by someone taller than she, using something hard and heavy. Struck repeatedly, cause of death skull fractures and resultant haemorrhage. The killer had been right-handed. The body had been found in the kitchenette. On the floor, a blood stain was the only reminder she had lain there. A tall stone bookend lay close to where she had fallen, but otherwise, there was no sign of a struggle. There had been no sexual assault nor evidence of consensual sex, which, to the two detectives, seemed out of the ordinary. Did it point to a woman as the killer? And there was the wine glass, curiously with two sets of fingerprints on it, neither of which were Rachel's.

The murder weapon was the horsehead-shaped bookend with a heavy, rectangular base. Rachel's blood was on it but there were no fingerprints or DNA residue other than hers. And as far as Rachel's cleaner could ascertain, nothing was missing from the apartment. It would seem, therefore, that the perpetrator had come prepared. The killer's motivation had not been robbery. An expensive diamond necklace and bracelet lay in the jewellery box on the dressing table. Rachel's wallet was still in her handbag and contained notes.

Importantly, there was no sign of forced entry. Time of death was put at between seven and nine o'clock the night before.

The detectives resumed their questioning of Michelle.

"Do you know anyone who would wish to harm Rachel Klein? Anyone from her past? A young man who she had broken up with, that sort of thing? I know it's difficult for you to think about that in relation to a good friend, but we have to ask."

"Well, men do fall in love with Rachel. Have you seen her? She's extremely beautiful." Michelle broke off, realising that the Rachel detectives had seen would have been a dead Rachel.

Composing herself, as best she could, she continued. "There was this this one boy at uni. He was pretty heartbroken.

But he never threatened her or stalked her or anything like that. And a couple when we were still at school. But we were just kids."

"We'll get those names from you before we leave. Anything else?"

Should she mention the university lecturer that Rachel had had a (fairly long) fling with in third year? She didn't want to blacken Rachel's name. He had been married. But this was the police. Would she be guilty of obstruction of justice if she kept things from them? She didn't know. Surely, they would be discreet anyway.

She decided to tell them. They took his name. Again, she said, Rachel hadn't said anything about any worrying behaviour.

"What about recently?" Copeland asked. "Had she been seeing anyone?"

Michelle had been dreading this. She hesitated again. She felt her face flush. Her hands were shaking a little.

"You know she's a paralegal, right? Well, she had been seeing the lawyer she works for — sorry, worked for. His name's Vincent. I don't feel very comfortable talking about it. He's married. To another lawyer. It was for about six months. She broke it off with him a couple of months ago. His wife didn't know. Rachel didn't break-up his marriage or anything. She wasn't like that." Michelle was unaware that she was now using the past tense in relation to her friend.

Rachel had by now, told her of her interest in Howard. She had begun seeing him. And she thought to herself that maybe, after all, Rachel *was* like that, despite what she (Michelle) had just said to the police. Maybe this time she (Rachel) would have been prepared to break up a marriage. Howard had the kind of money that she aspired to, the prestige, the drive, the whole package. And he already had children. He would not be pressuring Rachel to have more.

All of this ran through her mind now. She knew something else too, about Howard. He had been doing something a bit dodgy, to do with money laundering. Michelle hadn't been able to understand what exactly it was that he had done, but it had been shared between Vincent and Rachel while they had still been lovers. What was she to say to the detectives? How much of this would reach the newspapers, or the men's wives. None of this was relevant to Rachel's murder, she reassured herself, so there was no reason that it would be divulged by the police. She had better tell them all she knew. She was not used to being dishonest, but Rachel had always trusted her totally with her secrets. How could either of them have foreseen a situation like this?

"Ummm, this is probably nothing either. But Rachel has — had — seen a senior partner a couple of times since she had broken up with Vincent."

"Senior partner? You mean Howard Brookes?"

"I just know his name was Howard."

"And when you say 'seeing him', do you mean this was an intimate relationship?"

"Rachel didn't exactly say. That's all she said. That she had seen him a couple of times. It's not important, is it?"

"We have to follow up all information in a homicide case, Ms Hildebrande. It's just routine. You just need to tell us anything at all you know. It's up to us to judge what is or isn't important."

"Well, there is just one more thing. It's a bit weird and I don't see how it could relate to Rachel's death. It's just that she knew something about Howard and some money laundering for some clients. I really couldn't understand it. Something about setting up companies."

"And how did Rachel know about this?'

"Vincent told her when they were still together."

Pillowtalk.

"Is there anything else you can tell us about your friend, Ms Hildebrande? Anything at all, no matter how small?'

"No, I can't think of anything else. Only what a good friend she was and how much I miss her. Please find whoever did this terrible thing."

The detectives gone, Michelle reflected on the things she had revealed. She couldn't imagine that any of it had been of any help. Rachel's involvement with married men had always alarmed her, no matter how much love she had had for her friend. But Rachel was so loyal to her, such a dependable friend, and her relationships with men were her own business, after all. They were not given to judging each other. All that Michelle had told the police this morning couldn't possibly have any bearing on Rachel's murder. Murder! Such an unthinkable word to use in relation to Rachel, indeed to anyone in Michelle's ordinary, middle-class, uneventful life. It was a word that belonged to the newspapers, the television, not in the everyday of her existence. She felt again that sense of unreality, a detachment, as if she was observing events from a distance, not actually involved in them herself.

And, really, Vincent and Howard? She did not know them in person, but did know that they were highly respectable, law abiding, elite members of the community. The detective would not take long to erase them as irrelevant to their investigation. There was no reason that their wives would have to know. She had not caused anybody any trouble.

There was just one thing she had held back on. She was not sure why. Just some sort of instinct.

Rachel had talked to her about how hard Vincent had taken the breakup. She had been at first surprised, then irritated, and finally, just plain angry.

Vincent had confronted her in her office where he had ostensibly come to talk with her about some research for a case he was preparing for. He had wanted to know what was going on, was something wrong, when could he see her.

"Vincent, there's nothing wrong. It's been great. I've loved all the times we've spent together. But we've both known it couldn't last forever. You've got Gillian. It's just time to move on, that's all."

"Rachel, no. I need you. I can't lose you just like that. Please. It doesn't have to be as often. Just sometimes. Whatever suits you."

He was starting to seem pathetic.

"Vincent, it's over. Let's have happy memories to look back on. We'll still be friends. We'll see each other every day at work, still go for a drink sometimes, have a few laughs for old times' sake."

"Rachel, I'll leave Gillian if that's what you want. Anything. Just tell me. What do you expect me to do?"

"For God's sake, Vincent," she said. "Just stop acting like a love-sick schoolboy. It's pathetic. That's all I expect. It was good while it lasted, but it's over." And she turned sharply and walked away.

At that moment, he wanted profoundly for her to be dead. Reminiscent of Don Jose over the body of his beloved —

My Carmen, my beloved Carmen.

VINCENT

Vincent had been unnerved to receive a phone call asking if he would mind coming down to police headquarters at eleven tomorrow morning. Just more routine enquiries.

Detectives Copeland and Morrison had been over the summary of the autopsy results on Rachel Klein. The repeated blunt force trauma from behind, they knew about. The murder weapon was in no doubt. It was still stained with her dried blood. Fractures to her skull, epidural haemorrhage. Blood pooled around the body. There was a small amount of alcohol in the deceased's system but no drugs, illicit or otherwise. Specific tests had been run for those substances that required them. Stomach content analysis revealed partly digested lettuce, tomato, celery, red peppers and egg. All ingested approximately one hour prior to death. Time of death was estimated at around seven to nine on the evening before the body was found. There was no bruising to any part of the body. No bruising to the forehead meant she had crumpled to the floor, consistent with the position in which she had been found. No tissue under the fingernails, which led the two detectives to surmise that the first blow had been heavy and took her by surprise. She had had no chance to defend herself. No sign of a struggle. There would be no bruising or scratches left on the perpetrator.

As they knew, there was no trauma to the vagina or anus and no evidence of consensual intercourse or any bizarre sexual practice. She had had no warning of her imminent death. The detectives found some comfort in that. Hardened as they were, they both knew that the more you got to know about a victim, the more personal the work became, the more saddened you were. And the more anger you carried toward the perpetrator.

From their initial enquiries, they were approaching the case from the point of view of motive. Everyone knew that very often, the murderer was known to the victim, an intimate partner or family member (and there was no sign of forced entry). The killer was much more likely to be male and the motive for killing a woman was most often jealousy, revenge or concealment. For a female killer, it was predominantly about love or money. However, women have been known to kill for revenge.

Vincent was not familiar with police stations but this one did not resemble the American television version, a rundown, unpleasant and overcrowded, undefined space with tough cops jostling for position of Alpha male whilst tattooed, defiant, petty criminals were being hustled by. Vincent was ushered through to a reasonably pleasant office, offered tea or coffee by a young officer and a comfortable seat. His visions of being seated on a hard, wooden chair in the middle of a stark room lit by one dangling naked bulb, and being questioned by a cop of threatening affect, with rolled up shirtsleeves and loosened tie, vanished.

"Thank you for coming in, Mr Barnwell," one of the homicide detectives, Copeland, said.

Vincent, nervous, asked if they had any idea who harmed Rachel (he could not bring himself to use the word 'murdered').

"It's early days, sir," replied Morrison.

"We wondered if anything else had come to mind since we spoke to you," asked Copeland.

"No, it has just been a horror story. To all of us at the firm, even to anyone who knew her only slightly. But we've practically stopped talking about it. We were just going around and around the same circle. There's nothing more to say. I would have rung you if I had thought of anything else."

"We always follow up. Things can slip people's minds."

"Sir, you have explained that you had occasion to visit Ms Klein at her home to catch up with work you needed your paralegal for."

"Yes, just a few times."

"Could you tell us how many times?"

"Oh, I guess three or four."

"More precisely? Was it three or was it four?"

"I think four."

"Do you have a key to her apartment? A security swipe?"

"No. No I don't. She used her own keys to let us in."

Vincent began to sense a shift in the tone of the interview. Was this routine questioning? It was starting to feel a little like thumbscrews.

"Did Rachel Klein ever come to your home to work on legal matters?"

"No, it was easier at her place with no one else there. At my place, my wife would probably be at home."

"I see. And you don't have a study that you and Ms Klein could have used?"

"Well, I do. It's just a bit nicer after hours if you can spread out in the living room. You know what I mean."

"Was your wife aware that you sometimes worked back

with your paralegal?"

"Well yes, naturally. Of course I mentioned it. No reason not to."

"And sir, how would you describe your relationship with Ms Klein? Was it purely professional?"

"Yes, of course. Just professional. We had to work together quite closely." Nervous now. But who knew otherwise? Michelle crossed his mind again. Would Rachel have told her?

"You said that it had been about two or three months since you had last been at her home. You have not had occasion to work with her after hours in that time?"

"No. No not really. I haven't needed as much of her input recently. You know, it varies."

"Have you been intimately involved with Ms Klein at any stage?"

"No, absolutely not. She was simply my paralegal." He determinedly retained eye contact with the detective.

"Do you have a key to Ms Klein's apartment? Or have you ever?"

"No, never." Rachel had in fact, asked for his swipe and key back, at the office.

"Can you tell us where you were on the night of Wednesday, 10th October?"

"I guess you mean the night Rachel was killed. Why are you asking? Surely I'm not a suspect."

"Sir, we cover all bases. That's our job. It's the process whereby we eliminate people from our enquiries. Now, if you could tell us about that night."

"I know I was at home that night. Didn't go out at all."

"Is there anyone who can corroborate that? Your wife?"

"Gillian had stayed back at work. She was busy with a criminal matter she was working on. Gillian doesn't like bringing her work home. She'd rather stay back when it's necessary. She was there till about eight or so."

"Sir, you have been most helpful. Thank you again. There's just one other thing. Would you consent to being fingerprinted? And a saliva sample?"

Vincent hesitated for just a moment. But he could not see a problem. Of course, they would find his fingerprints in Rachel's studio, but that had been explained. And he could not see how his DNA could come into it.

"Whatever helps," Vincent replied, though never in his wildest dreams would he have imagined himself at a police station being fingerprinted. Hell, he could not have imagined himself being questioned by homicide detectives.

Vincent gone, Detectives Copeland and Morrison exchanged notes.

They knew that he was lying about having an affair with Rachel. But his silence could be explained by his not wanting his wife to know. He did not have an alibi. There was nothing extraordinary about that; it was just a factor. He was an upstanding, professional member of the community. But both men were hardened enough by experience to know that they did not automatically rule him out. Most murderers seemed perfectly normal up until the day they killed someone.

He did have a strong motive though. Rachel Klein had seemingly replaced him as her lover.

The fingerprints on the wine glass had the detectives puzzled. Why would there be two sets of fingerprints on the same glass, neither of them Rachel Klein's? Well, they would soon be finding out whether one set belonged to Vincent

Barnwell. Fingerprints had a long heritage. They had been used for identification in thousands of cases over time. There had been cases where the testimony of fingerprint experts had been almost the entire basis on which the defendant was found guilty.

How long could the glass have sat there, on the kitchen bench, unwashed? It had been six days since the cleaning lady had been, so that was the maximum time it could have sat there. That was hardly likely though. Just a glance around her small clean and tidy apartment was enough to tell you that. Most likely was that the glass had been used on the night of the murder and that Rachel Klein would have washed it and put it away the next morning, before that chance was so brutally and finally taken from her.

The detectives did not have to wait long. One set did belong to Vincent Barnwell. So, his story that he had not been to her apartment for around two months was entirely untrue. It seemed now that he had been there on the very night of her murder. His affair with Rachel Klein was over, if Michelle Hildebrande was to be believed. So why was he there? Was it for work purposes? If so, why did he deny that he had worked back with her in recent months? Perhaps, simply because his wife wasn't happy about it. Vincent had implied that she didn't mind. But it would be a very tolerant wife indeed who wouldn't mind her husband spending evenings alone with a woman who looked like Rachel Klein.

They could account now for one set of fingerprints, but whose were the others? One possibility was that they belonged to Vincent's wife, that they'd been at the deceased's apartment on the night of the murder for some reason. Then, once again, why in that case had Vincent denied being there? Could the two of them have conspired to kill her? Folie à deux. Not completely unheard of. And they could not come up with any alternative explanation. The other identical glass, also sitting there on the kitchen bench, carried only Rachel's fingerprints, as did the bottle, two thirds full of warm, white wine.

Together, the detectives agreed that they would talk to Gillian Barnwell next. She would probably know that they had spoken with her husband, first at his place of work and now at the station. According to Rachel's best friend Michelle, the wife had no knowledge of the affair. In the detectives' experience though, that was rarely the case; a wife was quite attuned to subtle changes in her husband's demeanour or behaviour. Or otherwise, some small thing tipped her off.

Then there was Howard to consider. The money laundering thing was odd but probably nothing to do with the homicide. They could alert Fraud Squad to that.

Suspicious minds.

GILLIAN

Gillian had no fear of being questioned. She had thought of everything.

Gillian had stayed back at work on the evening that Rachel had been killed. She had let two months lapse since their dinner party. There were always at least two lawyers working late. Tonight, Jim Parsons was down the corridor. He had stuck his head in and jokingly commiserated with Gillian about them being the lucky ones, before disappearing back into his office.

At about six forty-five, Gillian rang Vincent at home to say she would be home as soon as she could and would order takeaway for them both before she left. She then popped her head around Jim's door and said she was just going out for a 'proper' coffee and did he want one too. She knew only too well that he never drank coffee after four in the afternoon but wanted to account for her absence from the office if he happened to notice it, which was unlikely.

Leaving her computer logged on, and leaving her phone in her office, Gillian hurried across the road to the Grand Central Hotel which employed a barista until closing time. She made a point of chatting with him so that he would remember her, if ever she needed to rely on that.

She then walked, quickly, one block to the cab rank where she hopped in and asked the driver to take her to a spot around the corner from Happy Boy restaurant, a very short walk from

Rachel's small apartment block. She had been there just once before with a bottle of wine to welcome her to the firm just after she started.

There was no-one to see her. She rang the intercom. Rachel was surprised to hear that it was Gillian who was there but asked her to come on up. Gillian wiped the intercom keypad clean of fingerprints as the door unlocked. Rachel welcomed her in, invited her to have a seat.

Rachel seated herself, drink already in hand, in one of the comfy, green, tub chairs and looked expectantly at Gillian, inquiring but not nervous. Rachel had not broken up their marriage. It had all been just a fling.

Gillian looked good. She knew that. She looked after herself. She had not endured the ravages of pregnancy. No, her body was taut and her breasts still full and high. Her leisure time was not dominated by the needs of children, so she was not constantly harassed. She had the time to go to the gym almost daily. Trips to the hairdresser were frequent. She was beginning to have subtle treatment with Botox and fillers.

However, looking at Rachel now, she knew that no matter what she did, none of it could compete with being ten years younger. There was nothing quite like youth. The younger you were, the more fertile you were, the more attractive you were to the opposite sex. That was just a biological fact.

"The reason I'm here is that you work so closely with Vincent. He just hasn't been himself. He seems very down. Nothing I do seems to help. Have you noticed anything at work?"

"Just let me get us a drink. Then we can talk. White wine for you? I've got a bottle open. Just had a glass with dinner." Gillian had to admire her cool, unflustered demeanour.

Rachel stood and turned to the little kitchenette, which was only part of the living room, defined by a terracotta tiled floor whereas the rest of the room was carpeted. She opened her small refrigerator and took out a bottle of Pennavale Reisling which she had purchased on-line through a wine club. She then reached up for two wine glasses, put them on the kitchen bench and began to unscrew the bottle.

By this point, Gillian had picked up the heavy marble bookend that she had seen the only other time she had been there, when she had popped in with the gift of wine to welcome her to Vincent's corporate group. She walked up behind Rachel, all the while talking about her and Vincent's Christmas plans and preparations. She then lifted the seemingly innocuous bookend, now a weapon, as high as she could and smashed it down heavily on the back of Rachel's head. Rachel uttered an indecipherable sound and crumpled to the floor. Gillian bludgeoned her again and again.

Gillian then dropped the bookend and carefully wiped any blood from her hands on to Rachel's kitchen hand towel and put it carefully into a plastic bag in the top of her tote. She put on plastic gloves she had brought with her, took the wine glass out of her bag and put it on the bench and removed one of Rachel's wineglasses and dropped it into her tote too. Finally, she took five more matching wineglasses out and put them into the glasses cupboard to make up a matching set of six. She had made her set up to its usual eight at home too.

All was quiet outside. Gillian walked quickly back down to James St and took a cab to Central Station, minutes from work. Back at work, she noticed the light on down the hall in Jim's office, slipped into hers and logged off. She popped in to say goodnight to Jim and was gone.

She was home by eight and found Vincent watching television.

"So good to be home. How's your evening been, hon?"

"Fine, fine. Did you get everything done that you wanted to?"

"Yep, all done. I ordered some dishes from Chai Thai while I was driving home. Should be here any moment. Like a wine? I'd kill for one."

"I'll get them. You sit down. You must be tired."

Gillian actually felt exhilarated as she had back at home with her parents after Zoe had drowned. They had grieved terribly as she had known they would, but gradually she, Gillian, had become their world.

Vincent had been grieving for some time now. This had not escaped Gillian's notice. He seemed to drift through the day on automatic, doing what he had to do but without enthusiasm. Often when she spoke to him, he missed what she said, and she had to repeat herself. In the evenings, he sat in front of the television watching anything that came on. Sex was infrequent and mechanical.

He was not staying back at work any more. He said they were just not that busy at the moment. Gillian wondered how he was performing on the job, whether his partners were noticing. She wondered also what his relationship with Rachel was.

She knew that after tonight he would change again. His grief may worsen. He may feel some relief that he was no longer having to see Rachel every day. He may even be glad that she was dead, felt that she deserved it. He would be put through a great deal of anxiety as he came under the police spotlight, especially with his fingerprints being on the wineglass in Rachel's apartment.

Whatever lay ahead, Gillian would weather it, as she had with her parents. She would be the constant in his life, the one he could depend on. However long it took, she would weather it, knowing in the end all his love and attention would be hers. She had always been able to delay gratification, a sign of intelligence.

Rachel was dead. She was gone forever. He would not obsess over her forever. That might happen in novels, but in real life, he would need flesh and blood, fun and good times. Who knew? She might even ignore her good sense for once and give him that child he so wanted. His gratitude to her may very well equal his love for their child. *Their* child.

But she was reminiscing. About *that* night. Right now, she had to be in the present, answering questions, because two detectives were here questioning her.

The two detectives introduced themselves, thanked her for coming in, took her details and offered her tea or coffee.

"Ms Barnwell, as I told you on the phone, we have just a few questions regarding the death of Rachel Klein. She was your husband's paralegal. Did he speak much about her? Any enemies, for example?"

"None that he mentioned. It has all come as a terrible shock to everyone. Still hard to believe it's real. We're all very saddened." Gillian thought she must sound like a quote from 'Guide to Grieving for Imbeciles'. "He didn't say much about her personally. I know she was a valued assistant and that he found her to be an excellent para. Efficient. A good researcher."

"Did you ever know her to cause any problems at work? With your husband or any of the other partners?"

"No not at all. I have never heard of her behaviour being

anything but exemplary. Why do you ask? Have you heard otherwise?"

"Nothing like that. Just routine. Did she get on well with the other paralegals?"

"As far as I know. She was extremely busy during the workday. I'm sure they all were. It's a very busy practice. Whether the paralegals socialised after work, I couldn't say. Vincent never mentioned it."

"Did you ever know of Ms Klein mixing socially with any of the partners or associates at all?"

"Just the normal stuff. There was the occasional staff do. Very occasional."

"You have never heard of Ms Klein being personally involved with anyone from the firm?"

"I'm not sure exactly what you mean. If you mean romantically then no, Vincent has certainly never mentioned anything like that. And I'm sure Vincent would have told me if he'd known of anything."

"Does your husband ever stay back late at work?"

"Of course. Like every lawyer as far as I know. One or two evenings a week. And yes, Rachel Klein worked back too on occasions. It was necessary at times. It is often a joint effort."

"Have they ever taken that work to Ms Klein's home rather than the office? Or brought it to your home? You know, a little more comfortable."

"No never. It is always at the office. Vincent values professionalism. I think he would see it as less than professional to be at a paralegal's home. Or ours. He did of course, occasionally bring work home, but he preferred to do it in the workplace. We try to keep our home as a sanctuary from work."

"Yes, that is very understandable. Did you yourself ever have occasion to visit Rachel Klein at home?"

"No, we didn't socialise. Except, of course, at the occasional work get together as I said. But then it was really just exchanging pleasantries. We weren't close at all, but I found her to be very nice. Never went to her home though. In fact, I have only a vague idea of where she lives."

"Thank you. And lastly — and you understand we have to ask you this in a murder enquiry — could you tell us where you were on the evening of Rachel Klein's murder?"

"Yes, I know exactly. I was working back at the office 'til around eight or a little before. Jim Parsons can confirm that. He was still there when I left. Then I went straight home and had a takeaway dinner with my husband."

"Ms Barnwell, you have been very helpful. Thank you once again for your time"

A request for fingerprints and saliva sample and Gillian was free, with an alibi and no motive.

Little lies

RACHEL

Detectives Copeland and Morrison mulled over what had eventuated so far, who to believe and where to go next.

There was the question of the murder weapon. It would seem that the perpetrator had known that the bookend would be there, and therefore, had been to Rachel Klein's place at least once before. This did not necessarily mean it was anyone of significance in her life. It could be conceivably someone who had done some repair for her, had cleaned her carpets, answered an ad…

This led to a discussion about a favourite crime among Brisbane's detectives when they reminisced about past cases. This was the infamous 'Ether Man' of the 1960s, who left a trail of traumatised women across Brisbane after six increasingly, and at times, almost fatal sexual attacks in a ten month period. At times, insidious means were used to insinuate himself, seemingly innocently, into the lives of the women who were to become his victims. In the case of his Milton victim, he met his twenty-one-year-old victim when he answered her husband's newspaper ad for the sale of his car, and actually sat down with the woman and her husband in their living room. He learnt that the husband was always out on Tuesday nights, the night he chose for the attack on her. Most alarming perhaps, was that the perpetrator was finally identified as a seemingly ordinary, young, married man who worked for the State Government's Children's Department.

Could Rachel Klein simply have been the victim of something so random? Could her killer have attacked before? They would have to get their people on to researching past attacks on women, not only in Brisbane but more widely.

So, were they looking for a psychopathic killer with no personal link to Rachel Klein, who murdered for abnormal psychological motivations? Someone who had somehow insinuated themselves into her life and whom she would let into the apartment?

Or was it more likely the killer had closer links to her, and personal motivation for taking her life?

Vincent Barnwell had motivation. He had been discarded by her and replaced. They had no idea though how much she had meant to him, whether he'd been in love with her, obsessed by her, or whether to him it had just been a casual fling. Michelle Hildebrand, Rachel's close friend, had given them no insight into that. Perhaps she had mattered very little to him. They had no way of knowing.

His fingerprints had been on the glass in her apartment, however. They were most probably left on the night of the murder, or at the very most after the cleaner had last been. But they did not prove absolutely that he had been there on the fatal night. He did not have an alibi for that night, however. It would have been possible for him to have killed Rachel Klein and still have been home when his wife arrived home from work. The DNA results, when they got them back, may prove significant.

The other set of fingerprints did not belong to Gillian. They knew that now. So that put paid to their highly improbable folie à deux speculation. She did have a fairly watertight alibi also. Jim Parsons had confirmed that she had been there the whole time that she had indicated, and they had checked her computer for login and log off times.

They were sitting in the break room. At least the station now had a pod machine, instead of the old vending machine. Times did change and little by little, progress was made. Morrison made two coffees.

"We need to pin down that second set of fingerprints," he began. "The guys haven't found the same ones anywhere in the apartment, not on kitchen surfaces, not on the wine bottle, not on the murder weapon. Nowhere. That makes it very odd. I mean, how do you explain that? Barnwell's were everywhere; but that was to be expected. Strange though, that they were not on any kitchen surfaces at all. Nor were the unidentified fingerprints."

"Someone could, of course, have cleaned the kitchen surfaces before they left. We know it's common for perps to clean for fingerprints before they leave," said Copeland. "But then, why would they not have wiped over their glass as well?"

"Yes, odd. And to get in, the killer had to either have had their own swipe and key or have used the keypad at the entry. Her cleaner had her own keys, but I think we could rule her out."

"There were no fingerprints on the keypad or doorknob. That kind of rules out tradesmen who've done some work for her before. She would hardly have let them have keys to her place."

"Unless she was screwing one of them as well. Who knows with a piece like that? She seemed to spread herself around. Maybe she was getting repairs done for free. Or they could have wiped the keypad clean. Is that who the second prints belong to?"

"The contacts on her phone have been checked. We'll have that list re-checked. For any service men this time. Or any other boyfriend. Maybe someone else was screwing her and she didn't tell Michelle Hildebrande about."

"Vincent looks most likely at this point. He has motive. Though apart from the fingerprints, everything else is all just speculation. We have only her girlfriend's say so that Barnwell had been bonking her. And that's only because Klein told her so. She's never actually seen them together. Same with the big boss, Brookes. So, we've got no proof of her screwing either of them. But we'll see if there's a match to either of them when the DNA from the body comes back."

"That diamond necklace and bracelet are interesting too. Wonder where they came from. Seems unlikely that she bought them for herself, but we can go back through her credit card transactions. They don't look like antiques, not like some family heirloom. But we can talk to her parents again and to her girlfriend. One of them might know."

The thought of talking to Rachel Klein's parents again subdued them for a time.

"Why don't we take a ride out to the crime scene and look over it again?" said Morrison.

"What, right now?"

"Might get a feel for something. See something we missed. Can't hurt."

They took the fairly short drive to Rachel Klein's apartment, or at least what had been her apartment. It was still cordoned off to everyone but police.

Hers was a small boutique development from the 1990s. There was no onsite management, no CCTV. It was in a newly gentrified suburb in the Fortitude Valley precinct. It was first settled by Europeans around 1850 when migrants from England arrived. They had to build themselves bark and slab huts, until they could find jobs and move on to something better.

The area was, at that time, considered unattractive and also somewhat unsafe because of the risk of attacks by indigenous inhabitants increasingly resentful of the British settlement.

The suburb developed into a working-class area characterised by small, timber 'workers cottages', built very close together on narrow strips of land. These are now prized and sell at prices beyond the reach of most people, and are, one by one, being renovated into contemporary comfort while retaining their quaint, original style.

Now Fortitude Valley was a desirable residential centre boasting luxury apartment complexes and a dining, entertainment and retail mecca.

Rachel Klein's apartment was one block from the well-known James Street, a glittering strip of expensive restaurants, bars and hotels as well as designer shopping. She obviously had not yet been in a position to acquire one of the more luxurious apartments but was, the detectives were beginning to discover, a girl on the way up. Her studio, though, was pleasant and attractively appointed.

The two men couldn't help but be drawn to the stain in the kitchen area where the blood had pooled around Rachel's head and body. They thought of the body on the pathologist's table, the beautiful young woman whom they now knew to be highly intelligent as well. They remembered the look of anguish on her father's face when he was required to identify his only daughter's body.

They had the post-mortem photos.

Had she played a dangerous game, one which led to someone wanting her dead? And was that because of obsession, or jealousy, or just the needs of a psychopath?

"It struck me as a little strange that the two wine glasses were different. In the cupboard there were five of one type and three of the other. If you were pouring a glass of wine for someone and one for yourself, wouldn't you take two matching glasses out of the cupboard?" said Copeland.

"Only it seems she didn't take them both out. Her fingerprints were on only one of the glasses."

"You would normally take them both out of the cupboard at the same time, wouldn't you? And you'd think the person who'd do that would be Rachel Klein. To my mind anyway."

"Unless Rachel was already having a drink when the killer arrived, and she told them to get a glass too."

"Then you'd think they'd pour their own wine, wouldn't you? Especially if it was a man."

"That pretty much rules out a returning tradesman. She would hardly have poured them a wine, much less asked them to help themselves to a glass. Unless she was having an affair with them."

"Yes," said Copeland. "Seems an unlikely scenario. I keep coming back to Barnwell. But we must be careful of that old mistake of trying to fit the evidence to a person we have already decided is the guilty party. That mistake has sent many an innocent man to prison. We need to keep an open mind."

"Fingerprint evidence can be fabricated. We mustn't forget that. Planting a glass at a scene with someone else's prints on it, isn't exactly original. It's one possibility to consider here."

"But with *two* sets of *different* prints?" exclaimed Morrison.

"Puzzling, and they weren't *necessarily* left there on the night. Though it's hard to imagine that Rachel Klein had left a glass unwashed on the kitchen bench for even one day. I mean, did you see how neat the apartment was? There wasn't a thing out of place. And it seems she used the other glass on the night she was murdered. There was alcohol in her stomach."

"Most likely they were both used on the night. But we have DNA tests still to come back. It's one thing to plant prints or even DNA, but it's a different thing again, to take them away."

"Sure is. Miss one little thing and you're screwed."

"And killers don't always leave DNA. It's a gift when you've got it."

Gimme little sign.

HOWARD

"Mr Brookes, thank you very much for coming in. As you know, we are looking into the death of Ms Rachel Klein. Ms Klein was employed at your practice. We have a few questions about the nature of your relationship with her," Detective Copeland said.

"My relationship with her was purely professional. She was Vincent Barnwell's paralegal. He was the one who worked closely with her. If you are wondering whether anyone was any threat to her, she may have confided in him. I'm afraid I can't be of much help," Howard replied.

"I'll come straight to the point, Mr Brookes. Did you have more than a professional relationship with the deceased? Had you recently developed a more intimate relationship with her?"

"That's absurd. I really must object. Why on earth would you ask?"

"It has been suggested. By someone close to the victim. We need to follow up on everything when it comes to murder."

"Well, I strongly refute the suggestion. Just someone's word against mine. Malicious gossip."

Doth he protest too much?

"There were an expensive diamond necklace and bracelet in Ms Klein's possession," said Detective Morrison. "The case looks very much new. As does the jewellery. Can you tell us anything about that, sir?"

"No, of course not. And I am bound to say that I object to this line of questioning."

"Sir, we just want to alert you to the fact that we are able to go through you credit card records and cash withdrawals."

"I think that at this stage I might like to have a lawyer present," Howard Brookes said, a little less certain of himself.

Unlike many men in this type of situation, he didn't ask the detectives whether his wife really needed to know about any of this.

"That's your prerogative, sir."

Half an hour later, the interview was able to continue, criminal lawyer — his old friend, Thomas Strong — present.

Having conferred with his lawyer, Howard Brookes admitted that he had bought the jewellery. He had been in an intimate relationship with Rachel Klein for around two months. There seemed little point in denying it.

"Have you ever been to Ms Klein's apartment, Mr Brookes?" asked Copeland.

Brookes' lawyer told him that he did not have to answer, but his client chose to do so. He had not. And no, he did not have a key.

"Where were you on the night of Rachel Klein's murder, sir?"

He declined, however, on his lawyer's advice, to answer this or any further questions, including where he would get together with Rachel.

"We may be needing to talk with you again, Mr Brookes," said Copeland. "And if you don't mind, could you give us fingerprint and saliva samples, sir? We can get a court order, but the simplest thing might be to do it voluntarily."

Howard was shaken now. Back at Strong's office, he sat and put his head in his hands.

"Hell, Tom. Where is this going? Damn that diamond necklace. I've done nothing. The police are treating me like a suspect. For God's sake. Yes, I was seeing Rachel. I know that I'm not squeaky clean. But murder! Is this stuff all going to become public? What can I do?"

"Howard, try to calm down. I understand that this has come as a shock. But I don't think the police see you as a suspect. In fact, I'm sure they don't. They have a way of making people feel intimidated. All they have is that you were seeing the victim for a short time and that you had bought her some jewellery. Hardly evidence of murder. But they have to follow up on everything."

"I'm embarrassed about this Tom. I don't know what you must think."

"All I think is that you're human like the rest of us. Who am I to judge? No, all I am interested in is helping you legally if need be. But I'm sure that's not going to be necessary. Just tell me this, have you ever been inside Rachel Klein's apartment? Do you have a key?"

"No never, and no key."

"Well, that leaves you in the clear. As well as having no motive."

"What about the press though. What about my reputation, my kids?"

Strong noticed that he did not mention Ann but did not comment.

Howard thought about the tabloids and their appetite for the lurid:

PROMINENT LAWYER HAS AFFAIR WITH MURDER VICTIM

He imagined the press waiting for him outside his house with microphones and cameras. People hesitating to speak with him in the street. Having to face colleagues at work. All unthinkable.

"Howard, the police aren't going to release this to the media. They will only do that when they charge someone. And that's not going to be you."

Howard had been grieving for Rachel. He had found her irresistible and thought they had a future together. His marriage had long ago lost its lustre and they had seen their children through school. Rachel was beautiful as well as smart and ambitious. After twenty years of sleeping with Ann, of all those faithful years, Rachel's young, unsullied body drew him into a world of long-forgotten desire, pleasure, abandon. Obsession.

Now she was gone. She had been murdered. Murdered. That was not something that happened in his world. It still seemed unreal to him. And now another layer was being added to the grief. Fear. Fear of what lay ahead now that the police had him in their sights. Perhaps the fear outweighed the grief. The baseness of human nature never failed to astound him. Here the woman he loved, adored, had been killed in such an horrific manner and his concern was for himself. Perhaps the fatal flaw made so much of in literature, really did exist outside of fiction. Here he was, Howard Brookes, brilliant corporate lawyer, pillar of society, model of integrity, now involved in a murder investigation, all because of one flaw — his inability to resist temptation of a beautiful woman. Lust. One of the seven deadly sins. Would he, as Macbeth had so famously done, lose everything he had worked for, because of a single flaw? For to Howard, the respect and admiration of his peers and his children was everything.

Howard may have felt even less safe if he had known that Gillian had phoned Ann, to invite her to meet for a wine at Sixes and Sevens. Gillian had been making a point of strengthening their friendship ever since the dinner party. This had come as a surprise to Ann, but she had found herself enjoying it. Ann was not in the habit of going out for a wine at five-thirty in the afternoon. In her life, that was the time she began to prepare dinner for Howard and the family. Dinner was always home-made, except for the occasional restaurant outing. Howard didn't believe in Uber Eats or Menulog. That wasn't the kind of home he wanted for his children. That is why he wanted a stay-at-home wife. That was what they had agreed. Plus, there was dessert every night too. Howard liked his desserts. Also, home-made. Except on Sundays when he didn't mind just ice-cream with fruit.

Well, maybe it was time her life changed. Howard's certainly had. Gillian had tipped her off on the phone as to Howard's infidelity. She thought it was only fair, that Ann know. It may help to understand any unexplained behaviour changes in Howard. And anyhow, with Rachel dead, she did not have to worry about the affair. Don't blame Howard, Gillian had said. Rachel Klein had a reputation where other women's husbands were concerned. She was dangerous.

"Hi, Ann. So glad you could come. We don't do this often enough," said Gillian.

"Gillian. So nice to see you. I just don't get to do this sort of thing."

"Well, we'll just have to fix that. We women are supposed to be a sisterhood. Especially we wives from the practice."

Ann was feeling defiant. She hadn't even left a note for Howard. Damn him. Damn dinner. He wasn't a child.

"Let me get the drinks," Gillian said. "White wine? Chardy? Sav Blanc?"

"Sav Blanc. Thanks."

Ann looked around at the crowd while Gillian was gone. The women were so well-dressed, designer stuff. A lot of them were younger, but when had she ever had a chance to enjoy herself like this? And there were women her age too. Well, her life might be different now. And so might Howard's.

Gillian came back with the drinks. "This looks like a nice one. Margaret River. Here's to us!"

"Totally. Look, thanks for filling me in on what was happening. It's hurting of course, hurting like hell, but I'd rather know what I'm dealing with," Ann answered.

"I'm relieved to hear that. It was really a hard decision for me to make. I didn't want to cause you pain, but I thought you should know. Otherwise, you're just being made a fool of. You deserve to know."

"Howard *has* been making a fool out of me, that's for sure. Working back late! And me having dinner ready for him no matter what time he got home. I understand now why he was always so preoccupied of late. I thought it was just that he still had work on his mind."

"Are you going to confront him about it?" enquired Gillian.

"I've been thinking about that. I'm not sure. I'll see how things go. You know, I'm feeling sad but I'm feeling a lot of anger too. Men. You have their children, then spend your life bringing them up and supporting their career. And then someone younger comes along, and this is what they do. I'm wondering if he would have left me for her."

"I don't think that would have happened. From what I hear, she moves on to the next one. Might have just lasted longer with Howard, to help her career along. Did you know she was studying Law? I just found out recently."

"So, our 'Fluffy' wasn't so fluffy after all. Tell me, how did you find out? Is it all around the practice?"

"Vincent hasn't said anything. I really don't think so. I happened to see them together one night, just by chance, going into the Calile. Obviously more than friends. Sorry you have to know that."

"Yes, well. Would you like another drink? I'll get them. A plate of snacks too. You're not in a hurry, are you?"

Gillian was satisfied. She was getting revenge on Howard as well. Any man who'd done this to their wife. Especially with bitch Rachel. And maybe there was more to Ann than they had all thought. Ann was settling in for a few drinks. Her phone was switched off. She was not planning on ringing home.

She knew where Howard filed their credit card statements. He still preferred hard copies. Normally she didn't bother looking at them. Perhaps it was time she did.

The carnival is over.

GILLIAN

The second set of fingerprints had come back. They belonged to Howard Brookes. They were still waiting on the DNA.

"So, we have both Barnwell's and Brookes' prints on the same glass. And only the deceased's on the other. Interesting. "What explanation do we have for that?" says Morrison.

"Well, it's been a couple of months, according to Barnwell, since he's been to her apartment. It's possible that the fingerprints have lasted that long," replies Copeland.

"Possible, but not all that probable. It could happen, maybe if she had just rinsed the glass, and let it dry on the drainer. She would have to be a pretty sloppy housekeeper. And then the glass just sits in the cupboard for the next two months without anyone using it."

"And she would have had to put it away and her prints would be on it. It's hardly likely that Barnwell would have put it back in the cupboard."

"Or Barnwell was there close to the murder or during it. Which he denies."

"Same for Brookes. Though he claims he has never been to Klein's apartment."

"And his fingerprints weren't found anywhere else, just on the glass."

"Yes, if they'd been having their tryst there, he'd have had to have left prints somewhere, you would expect. He couldn't have wiped them all off. Although, fingerprints aren't *always* left behind."

"I still haven't discounted the idea of the glass being planted. I know it sounds a bit fantastical. And a glass being planted is a touch Hollywood, but the idea that the two hombres used the same glass, in the apartment where the murder takes place, is a bit difficult to explain also."

"But who would have done it? And why? To frame someone else for a murder that they had committed? Maybe if there was just one set of prints. But two. How would they have gotten them? And why would they want *two* sets?"

Gillian, of course, knew exactly why. Yes, naturally she wanted to deflect culpability from herself. But as for the two sets — there was method in her madness. She wanted Vincent to suffer for a while. Like her parents had had to suffer after Zoe's death. They suffered from grief. They suffered from shame and ostracisation. All of this served to make Gillian the centre of their world. She became the one person they could always turn to. And so, it would be with Vincent.

If not for you.

At the same time, she didn't want him to go to prison. She did not want to lose him. He would suffer the anxiety of police interrogation. His life, like that of her parents, would take a turn that they never have foreseen. But in the end, it was all for the best. The police would almost certainly not charge Vincent. There was too much conflicting evidence. And in the unlikely event that they did, no jury would convict; the facts would be too confusing to allow them to decide 'beyond reasonable doubt'.

It's surprising just how easy murder is. The first murder

— Meg — seemed to have been so simple, an object quietly drawn under swollen water with scarcely a ripple. The second one was easy too but so different. I didn't know why, but I had not thought about the blood. That must sound naïve, but when we think about a blow to the skull, it doesn't seem to conjure up visions of blood. It's just a dull klunk and somehow, the person is unconscious. A few more klunks, and they're dead. But there was so much blood. A growing pool. As Lady Macbeth marvelled -

Who would have thought the old man to have so much blood in him?

Perhaps that should have alerted me. But then Hollywood doesn't prepare us, does it? Vincent and I just saw 'The Gentlemen" — life must go on, as they say. Well, one gentleman was shot in the middle of his forehead. The only sign was a clean bullet hole. No blood at all.

I have since found out why head injuries bleed a lot. It's all the blood vessels. The brain requires a tremendous amount of oxygen to do its job. In fact, about twenty percent of the blood flowing from your heart goes up to your brain. Other organs in your head, such as your eyes, also require a steady supply of oxygen-rich blood cells to work well.

Lying in bed at night, I view this little documentary. It seems to play in slow motion and I am audience to every little detail — the unique sound of marble on bone, the silent, almost graceful, crumbling of body to floor, the bright red fluid seeping into caramel hair, the growing pool of blood. The replaying is as devoid of emotion as the original event itself. The thrill that I felt afterwards though, the exhilaration, is now absent, disappointingly so. An air of unreality surrounds it all.

Somehow, in the planning and finally in the doing, it

seemed the easiest thing in the world.

What is thinkable is doable.

*It's interesting, isn't it, also, how you never know who among you is a murderer, **the** murderer. It can be anyone, could be the girl next door.*

The press had not lost interest either.

KILLER STILL AT LARGE

Homicide detectives are investigating the brutal 7th October murder of law student and paralegal Rachel Klein, twenty-four, whose body was found in her Fortitude Valley studio apartment.

Robbery does not appear to be a motive. Police are questioning persons of interest. The murder of a promising young student, of prominent legal firm Brookes, Taylor McCoughlin, is being viewed as a tragic loss of a prodigious talent and loving sister and friend.

Those close to Ms Klein describe her as vivacious and selfless. "She will be missed by all whose lives she touched, always put others first," a close family member said this morning.

Why was it, Gillian wondered, that anyone who died 'in tragic circumstances' (though when exactly was a death *not* tragic?) was without fail, selfless and giving, someone who 'touched peoples lives', who would be 'sadly missed'?

Though they *did* touch people's lives, through the media, the lives of strangers. It was they, the strangers, who really mourned her — or what they thought was her — with a grief that was no less sharp for not having known her.

Gillian had not known Rachel intimately, but still

marvelled at accounts in the media of her selflessness, given her penchant for other women's husbands and the apparent ease with which she could discard them. Rachel was not, either, a woman whom she could imagine working at the Neighbourhood Centre for the less fortunate or the breakfast van for the homeless.

Women's organisations had already waded in, using Rachel Klein's death to expose the violence against women's plight.

"If a woman cannot feel safe in her own home, then she cannot expect to feel safe anywhere," said one advocate.

Would she become a poster girl?

Rachel Klein?

Material Girl?

VINCENT

The forensics results had given Detectives Copeland and Morrison quite a lot to think about.

The DNA results were back. There was no saliva DNA. All they had was touch DNA, belonging to both Barnwell and Brookes.

There was a theory that juries notoriously only need to hear the word DNA to deem the defendant guilty, although juries were becoming more sophisticated in this regard. DNA evidence was, in reality, much less reliable and objective than most people think. It can be unequivocal under ideal conditions — when there is a large quantity of a suspect's well-preserved genes, when it's clear how the DNA arrived at the crime scene, and when the lab sequencing the sample doesn't make any mistakes.

"The fingerprints were probably left at or not long before the murder. Unfortunately, as you know, research on fixing the age of a fingerprint has a fair way to go. Opinion of experts about the age of fingerprints is seen as unreliable and is inadmissible in court," said Copeland.

"It's unlikely they had been there longer than the last cleaner's visit at the very most though. Unless she just rinsed and didn't wipe," replied Morrison.

"Cops have to be bloody scientists these days."

"Yeah, we know not to rely on touch DNA too, on pillowslips and so on, either. It spreads from one person to another too easily apparently. Like just through shaking hands. Tiny amounts can place people at locations they have never visited by transferring to the perpetrator to someone else and then to the scene. Easily shot down in court. Well, you know as well as I do, the defence would have a field day with it."

"So, who? Barnwell or Brookes?"

"Barnwell has a motive. Klein had given him the heave-ho and was now screwing Brookes. Men have killed over jealousy before. In fact, it is one of the most common motives. We both know that. And Brookes doesn't have a motive. Hell, he's been buying her expensive jewellery from Tiffany. Making more money than us, that's for sure."

"Barnwell seems like the likely one. He doesn't have an alibi either."

"But why leave *his* prints on the glass as well. He wouldn't be that sloppy, surely? And how would the glass match the others in Klein's cupboard? Coincidence?"

"People make mistakes. We know that. This is not someone who is used to committing crime. Certainly not murder. Might have got a fit of nerves. We've seen mistakes more stupid than this before. Can't explain the glass though, being part of a matching set, if it was planted. Damned if I can."

"It's not necessarily either/or here. A third party could have planted the glass. Another boyfriend we don't know about? One of the wives? Women do kill out of revenge or hate."

"Yeah, but as far as we can find out, neither of them knew that their perfect husband was servicing the lady. Still don't."

"Seems to be the case. And we can't prove otherwise. Anyway, where would they have got the glass from?"

"Could have been at a work event or a bar with the two of

them. A bit hard to imagine but not impossible. Hard to sell to a jury though."

"Yeah, would sound a bit like fiction, a bit of a stretch. And how would you explain how the glass got to Klein's kitchen bench?"

"We'd better have another chat with both men again."

Vincent was finding that being a suspect in a murder investigation inflates the imagination and its powers of invention astronomically. He had been lying awake at night wondering whether his DNA might be on all sorts of things, including the murder weapon. He has been reading up on forensic investigations. He had read about touch DNA. Damn Google. What a little knowledge can do to our anxiety levels.

What if he, Vincent, had transferred his DNA to the killer who then left it on Rachel's clothes or on the murder weapon on the night she was murdered? While this, he knew rationally, was highly unlikely, these kinds of thought could run rampant through your head when you are tossing and turning at two or three in the morning, unable to sleep. Possibilities would spring to mind, one upon the other, one no sooner rationalised then another would take its place. He would be reminded that his fingerprints would probably be all around the apartment, on door handles, on furniture. He had explained that, he told himself. He and Rachel had used her apartment to continue working after hours. The detectives suspected him of having an affair with Rachel Klein. Her friend, Michelle Hildebrande had probably told them that, probably told them that she had ended the affair too. That gave him motive. But they didn't have any proof. That was just hearsay. Only Rachel could have told her that and, as Rachel was now dead, she would obviously not be a witness in a courtroom. And any phone records on his phone or hers could be explained as work related.

How his mind was working overtime. How he tried to convince himself that he did not have anything to worry about. The anxiety, however, remained.

If only he could discuss it with Gillian. His wife was a highly-respected, criminal lawyer. She was always the one he turned to, always his support. Why had that not been enough? He had had it all.

He had a beautiful, clever wife who loved him and was so easy to live with. They had a good sex life. What was it about Rachel? The allure of her had become an addiction. How else could he explain it, even to himself? Her body, the smoothness of her, her sensuous lips, the nape of her neck when her hair fell away. Since he married Gillian, while he was aware of the allure of other women, he had been able to dismiss it as now *verboten*. It had never been a difficulty for him, as it was for so many men. Perhaps he even enjoyed knowing that he was capable of resisting. He was a mature man, he was a married man. He had been proud of his standing as a person of values, his partnership with Gillian, their closeness and hopes for his future. Rachel Klein had brought him unstuck. Somehow, she had brought him undone, with a glance, a look lasting a moment too long, until bit by bit he could think of nothing but her, care about nothing except their next assignation.

How could he have succumbed to such teenage obsession, lost sight of everything of value in his life? Since she had left him, he had allowed himself moments of breaking down, alone, weeping, head in hands, pitying himself, now that she was gone forever. He was not altogether sure what he was weeping for. Loss of Rachel? He didn't think so. He felt a strange relief now that she was dead. He had done his grieving over Rachel Klein. If he still wept, it was for the potential for loss of everything else.

Now, he thought, if he could come through this unscathed, he promised his God, he would never be unfaithful to Gillian again. All he wanted now was his old, peaceful, tidy life back, as it used to be.

If I could turn back time.

It was odd that he had been unable to break his addiction as long as Rachel had been alive. Now, after two painful months since the affair had ended so coldly, culminating in her death, he was cured. He had gone 'cold turkey', he supposed, and come through.

Now for the first time in his life, Vincent knew fear. Fear that he was alone with. There was no one at work he could talk to. It was not possible to speak to anyone about his affair with Rachel. If this ever did go to court, they could be called in as a witness against him. He was doing his job, somehow, running on automatic, with a new paralegal, a young male this time. Of course, at home, he could not open up to Gillian either. He had thought about it. She could not be made to testify against her husband. What, though, could he tell her? That the police seemed to think he had a motive for killing Rachel? That he had been to her apartment a number of times, so that he and Rachel could continue working, and he had never bothered to mention it? The last thing he wanted was to hurt her.

Perhaps he could confide in his father? Of course, his parents had been shocked and horrified by the murder and had found it as impossible to absorb as anyone else. That something like that could touch his son's life was almost unbearable to him. He could only imagine what it would do to his father if he confessed his infidelity or that the police had questioned him in the way they had. And his mother? That was unthinkable.

He and Howard had called on Rachel's parents, Stan and Helen Klein, to offer condolences on behalf of everyone from the firm. There is a special word in Sanskrit that means 'against the natural order'. It is 'Vilomah'. Our children should not precede us in death. 'Vilomah' is a name for the grief of bereaved parents. Visiting the parents of a dead child was something Vincent did not ever want to experience again. For a parent to lose a child is something that is almost impossible to make sense of. Howard was a parent himself. He did not even want to imagine how Rachel's parents must feel. Even though Vincent was not in their shoes, he knew it was not how the world was meant to be and that it was beyond comprehension. That was all he and Howard could think to say — "We can't begin to imagine... we are sorry... please accept out condolences on behalf of everyone at the practice..."

Howard had spoken at the funeral. His presence, as always, was commanding. The church grew completely still as everyone present waited on his words. He spoke gravely of the loss of a promising, young life, of its inexplicable end. He did not speak of the celebration of a life. Rachel's life had not yet been lived, had barely begun. He spoke of sorrow of the people in her life, of the joy she would have continued to bring them, of her enthusiasm and promise, of a mesmerising flame that had been extinguished far too soon. When he strode back to his seat, the gathered mourners did not stir.

How easily then Rachel's body was returned to ashes. Was Gillian the only one who secretly rejoiced? She thought not.

Someone had chosen a song —

Seasons in the Sun.

HOWARD

"Mr Brookes," said Detective Copeland, "there are one or two things we would like to clear up."

"I have advised my client that he is not obliged to answer any questions," his lawyer interjected.

"That is certainly the case. However, it may be in Mr Brookes' best interest to do so," Copeland replied.

"What is it you want to know?" asked Brookes.

"Can you explain how your fingerprints came to be on a glass, a wine glass, in Ms Klein's apartment on the day after her murder?"

"I strongly advise you not to answer, Howard," Thomas Strong said.

"No, I want to. I want to answer that. This is absurd. I have never been inside her apartment. Not ever."

"You have at some point drunk from that glass," continued Copeland. "Your fingerprints make that conclusive."

Thomas struggled to absorb what the detective was saying, the impossibility of Howard's fingerprints being on a glass in Rachel's apartment. This could not be happening. Howard felt removed, a sense of being apart from what was occurring around him. "That's impossible. As I've just said, this whole thing is utterly absurd. There must be some mistake," said Howard.

"There is no mistake, sir. Again, is there any way you can explain your fingerprints being on a glass in Rachel Klein's apartment?"

"No, of course I can't explain it. Someone must have planted it. Or maybe Rachel took it home with her after we had been together. Really, how should I know?"

"Can you tell us then, sir, where you were on the night of the murder?"

"Yes, I was at home with my wife, all night."

His lawyer interjected again, warning him about answering any more questions. At this point, Howard co-operated with him, feeling with a sense of panic that he was somehow getting out of his depth.

How could this be happening to him? Only a short while ago, he had been leading a safe, normal life, a family man, a highly regarded and respected figure in the legal profession. His marriage may have become stale, but he could sleep at night. Now, unbelievably, he found himself on the wrong side of the law.

What if the police spoke to Ann, found out that he had gone out for a while on the night of Rachel's murder? He had gone to visit his mother for a while as she had a few things she wanted him to see to. He had probably only been gone an hour. He remembered leaving his phone on the charger, deciding that he wouldn't need it. Maybe he would have to ask Ann for her help with his alibi.

Detectives Copeland and Morrison had by now examined Brookes' credit card activity. They had discovered a nine-thousand-dollar debit to a jeweller as well as six payments, each for a night's accommodation at the Calile Hotel. The debit for the jewellery was the most recent of these.

They now spoke to Ann Brookes. She had now also gone through their credit card statements. Those for the last two months were missing. It was a joint account. She could easily obtain copies. She was somewhat shaken by the questions the detectives had asked, but had told them that her husband had little contact with Rachel Klein, he never mentioned her private life and that he had been at her home with her on the night of the murder. The night stood out to her, she said, because she and Howard had watched the overly-long movie 'The Irishman' on Netflix. Ann may have been angry and resentful towards her husband, but she still did not want any police interest in them or her home.

Howard had been struck by the recent sudden change in his wife. He knew she had forged a relationship with Gillian Barnwell and supposed that explained her newly acquired independence, her changes in behaviour, being less and less at his beck and call. He didn't mind actually. Her not always being home so predictably gave him some 'me time', for one thing. But it was more than that. After being so in love with Rachel, he knew that he couldn't settle for what he and Ann had, not indefinitely, not forever. He would have to leave her. He had never wanted a broken home, he never thought it would happen to him, but now knew that he had to find again the passion and thrill that he had experienced with Rachel.

Ann and Gillian were having another get-together, this time at Felons. They shared concerns about having been questioned about their husbands' knowledge of Rachel Klein's private life and their whereabouts on the night of the murder.

"I suppose they talk to anyone with a connection to the victim when it's a case of murder," said Gillian. "It's funny, I'm a criminal lawyer and I know the law about murder as well as court procedures, but I know very little about police investigation protocol," she said.

"Yes, I just wondered why they asked about Howard's whereabouts. I suppose it means they somehow found out about their affair. But that's hardly evidence of murder. I mean, it doesn't give them a motive," said Ann.

"Unless they're thinking she might have been threatening to tell you. I don't know. It's just a thought. Although I don't see how they could even know about Howard and Rachel. I have no idea why they asked about Vincent though. Just because she was his para, I suppose."

"Yes, he *is* the person who worked most closely with our Fluffy. I suppose they cover all bases and he would have to be included."

"What motive could Vincent possibly have though?"

"Well, that's the thing. He doesn't have a motive, so they'll have eliminated him pretty quickly."

"There's one other thing, Ann. I really don't want to give you anything else to worry about, but Howard asked Vincent to ask my advice on something a little while ago and it's probably best for you to know. Apparently, Howard is worried that he might have been instrumental in facilitating money laundering for some client. Setting up shelf companies. Common practice for corporate lawyers. I told Vincent that I really don't think Howard has anything to worry about. I'm not Howard's lawyer so I'm not bound by confidentially. So, I can tell you."

"And you really don't think he has done anything wrong?"

"Nothing criminal anyway. I suppose ethics is another matter."

"You haven't told anyone else, have you?"

"Of course not. Ann, the reputation of the firm is just as important to me as it is to our husbands. And please don't let

Howard know I've told you. It's just between ourselves."

Ann arrived home to find Howard was there, earlier than normal. He had something he wanted to talk to her about, urgently.

"Ann, I'm sure it's only routine, but I had two detectives asking me a few questions about Rachel Klein this afternoon. Whether I knew of anyone who might want to harm her, that kind of thing. They asked where I was on the night of the murder. I told them I was at home with you. I didn't see any need to say I had popped over to mum's place for a while. No point in telling them that. It's just if police ask you, could you back me up on that?"

"As a matter of fact, two detectives did ask me a few questions this afternoon, Copeland and Morrison? Are they the ones who spoke with you?"

"Yes, that's them. Did they ask about where I was on the night?"

"Yes, I told them you were here all night. I didn't mention you going out. I said the night stood out in my mind because we'd watched such a long and standout movie, 'The Irishman', on Netflix."

"Thank God. Thanks for that, really."

"I'm not even sure why I didn't tell them," remarked Ann. "Just some kind of instinct. So, now I've lied to the police. But why are you worried about having an alibi? There's absolutely no way they could suspect you."

"Of course not. I'd just like to have all bases covered, just in case. You never know what could eventuate in a case like this. You know me, the perfectionist. You can't be too careful. Everyone concerned is a suspect. What else did the police ask?"

"Only whether you had any personal contact with Rachel.

I told them, no. That's right, isn't it?"

"Yes, I had very little to do with the poor girl. I know that Vincent found her very good as a paralegal, that's all. I was unaware she was studying at the university."

"Such a loss. The practice will be poorer without her," Ann said, with feigned sadness in her voice.

When first we practise to deceive

ANN

Ann had been seeing a psychiatrist for some years now, to deal with clinical depression. She had talked to Dr Susan Matthews about her feelings of lack of purpose. She had, as she and Howard had agreed early on, devoted herself to bringing up the children and caring for the home while he earned the money, very good money, to support them.

Even during those years as the children went through school, she felt desperately that she would like to study, go to university, and make something more of herself. Home on her own, she had pored over options in the tertiary admissions course guide. She was drawn to Computer Science. She found the thought of learning to program exciting. She fulfilled the requisites to gain entry. She had felt a growing exhilaration at the prospect.

Ann had been a bright student at secondary level. Her parents though, had not encouraged her to seek university entry when she had completed school and she had always been meek and submissive, always trying to please. Her brothers, they had said, would have to support families and needed a university education. They were not financially well-off and having to support Ann through three or four years of university as well would put so much strain on them.

When Ann had left school, she had enrolled in a short bookkeeping course in which she had excelled and had no difficulty in finding a job.

Now, at age forty-three, excited, she had broached the idea of going to university at last, with Howard. He was incredulous.

"What on earth for? Computer Science? At the University of Queensland? You'd never compete with today's eighteen-year-olds. They've grown up virtually attached to computers. You'd make a fool of yourself."

"Howard, you know I was very good at IT subjects when I was at school. I picked up the basics of programming easily."

"Even so. And what about the kids? It's not what we agreed upon. They have their university years ahead of them. They'll need all the support they can get. Be here for them. Help with assignments. Look, tutor *them*. That should be fulfilling if you're looking for fulfillment."

And so, Ann capitulated. Again.

Dr Mathews had talked to her about her need to please. This could spring from childhood experiences. It was particularly common in women.

She talked to Ann about her options. Insisting on enrolling at university would almost certainly lead to Howard's being resistant and unpleasant. They talked about ways of dealing with that and how eventually things would get better.

But it had all seemed too much and Ann had taken the easy path and put her own needs last. She had continued to battle with her depression.

Now, ten years later, the children grown up, and knowing of Howard's infidelity, his credit card charges for jewellery and the Calile Hotel, Ann had changed. She no longer felt a need to please. On the contrary, she felt angry and rebellious. She knew that Howard had sensed that; he would hardly have failed to. He wouldn't dare try to squash her, tell her that she was too old, that it was pointless, that so many women would give anything to have what she had.

You don't own me.

Dr Mathews encouraged her. Lots of people started university courses in mature age, she said. She told Ann of a doctor friend who was now in her second year of a law degree.

She asked Ann how she would cope if Howard was again resistant. She was surprised when Ann replied that she did not care and that she had made up her mind this time.

"I'm so pleased for you, Ann," said Dr Mathews. "You've wanted this for a long, long time. But I must add that you will need strategies in place in order to be assertive without your marriage becoming a battleground. We can talk about that."

The psychiatrist knew, of course, about Rachel Klein's murder and her connection to Howard's practice. It had been all over the media.

Ann did not tell her psychiatrist however, about Howard's liaison with Rachel. Howard had been questioned and so had she. While knowing that Howard had had nothing to do with Rachel's death, it was a murder investigation and she was fairly sure that psychiatrists were bound to inform the police if they knew that a client had been involved in a murder. That fell outside the doctor-patient confidentially arrangement. Whatever the case, she felt that it was better that she didn't mention Howard's affair.

Ann and her doctor had, over a long period, addressed her childhood trauma. She and her little brother, Sam, had been playing on the lawn in the front yard of their suburban home.

She had been eight years old and he only four. They were not playing with a ball. They were trying handstands and somersaults. They were never allowed to have a ball in the front yard even though the street was a cul-de-sac and there was very little traffic. Their mother had been checking on them at intervals.

Then the quiet, uneventful street, became, in an instant, a scene from a horror movie, played in slow motion. Across the road Sam saw the neighbour's dog, who he loved to play with. He called, "Roxy!" and without even a pause, he darted across the street. Too late. Ann cried, "No Sam," and reached to grab him. She was on her feet running after him, arm stretched to full length. She saw it happen, frame by frame. Sam's little legs, running. The car, brakes screeching, colliding with the excited little boy. The tiny figure tumbling in the air. The body sailing across the bonnet and smashing into the windscreen. After that, things seemed to speed up. People emerged from doorways everywhere, someone huddling over the too still Sam, the driver of the car frantic, distraught. And the little boy's mother crying, screaming out, "No, no, no."

Someone remembered Ann, ushered her inside, wrapped their arms around her. She did not see the ambulance arrive or take Sam away. She never saw him again, only his little white coffin at his funeral.

The psychiatrist had told her that she was fortunate to have had parents knowledgeable enough to have found a very good therapist for her following the traumatic event. That is probably why she had not endured a lifetime of post-traumatic stress disorder. This disorder was no longer seen as limited to the experience of war. Ann did still exhibit symptoms of depression, but there were other reasons for that, including not having fully resolved her grief for the loss of her brother and they still had to address that. Dr Mathews had engaged her in treatment.

Ann could not have complained about Howard's support of her through all of this. Howard, as usual, did the upstanding thing. She had been grateful to him, and in return, tended to give in to his wishes. She had not wanted arguments, wanted above all a harmonious home.

Now that she had learned about Rachel, as hurt and angry as she was, she had to admit that she still had no desire to break up the marriage. What would that achieve? She had no wish to live alone. She could not even imagine becoming involved with other men. And the property settlement! She loved their beautiful Hamilton home, a charming colonial which they had so carefully restored. She tried to imagine selling her home and found the thought unbearable. The children had grown up there. She thought of their future grandchildren, of them playing on the same swings, squealing happily in the same swimming pool, kicking a ball on the same green lawn. She thought of sitting on the wide verandahs watching them.

It was unthinkable that they should sell the home that meant so much to her, buy separate places that could never be as big or as lovely, go their own ways. She would receive a decent financial settlement but she knew, realistically, that her standard of living would be reduced. And that would be forever.

Yes, she was angry. But Rachel was gone. Gillian was right. It wouldn't have lasted. Rachel tempted men, they found her hard to resist, she got tired of them and moved on. Howard had not really loved Rachel, she believed. He was still with her, Ann, wasn't he? She was the one he truly loved. It had just been temporary. Things would not go back to being the same.

She would have her university study, her new liberating friendship with Gillian. Howard would get used to it. Their dynamic would change. She would probably not ever totally forgive him, but it was out of character for him and he was more than likely regretting it, already over Rachel, realising the kind of person she had really been.

Whatever the future held though, Ann knew now that she had two very supportive and intelligent women who would be with her through it. She had Gillian and she had Susan Matthews, two people she could always talk to. Ann could not have foreseen the massive impost that the interaction between the childhood trauma she had experienced and the intervention of these two extraordinary women would have on her life.

Lean on me.

VINCENT

Here the detectives were, two men in a city of two million, charged with the responsibility of dealing with yet another homicide committed here, finding another perpetrator and the evidence required to prosecute and convict them.

They were in the Drawing Room Bar of the historic, and faithfully reproduced, Gresham Hotel, now situated in the iconic Queensland National Bank Building, in the city centre, discussing this latest case, one that had gripped the public's attention and demanded an answer. Their gracious surroundings belied the brutality of the events that they had been pondering. Murphy's Creek sandstone and New Zealand limestone lined the walls. A Palladian influence was evident in the detailing. Local cedar formed the doors and joinery. The mantelpiece above the fireplace was made from marble sourced from the United Kingdom. They sat facing each other, the old maple coffee table separating them. The ceiling soared above them, cornices finely detailed, centred with a decorative rose from which hung a wrought iron chandelier. Sepia prints of earlier times graced the walls. The only other patrons were two couples engrossed in conversation in the corners of the room, oblivious to the two men with their tired, worn faces, whose business was the unfortunates who had met a violent and untimely death at the hands of one of their fellow man.

The cool of the dim, airconditioned room provided respite from the relentless, baking summer heat. For months now, the media had provided constant reminders of blazing bushland and lives and properties lost, as fires raged along the full length of the vast drought-ravaged eastern side of the Australian continent. The drought conditions and fires had caught the attention of the entire world.

Strangely, though, it was not enough that nature, unforgiving as it could be, had randomly taken lives too soon. Man had taken an even greater number of lives, deliberately and with purpose. And one of these lives had been that of the young, beautiful and talented Rachel Klein. These two seemingly ordinary men, faced the extraordinary task of deciding who was responsible and why, and providing the wherewithal to convince a jury, that they had indeed offered up the right defendant.

Other men's jobs involve the business of healing the sick, teaching the young, managing money, offering hospitality. So many occupations that they could have chosen, yet the occupation that they had chosen was violent death. Through years of the iniquity that they had faced together, Copeland and Morrison had developed a bond like no other. The fraternity of the police force was unique. It seemed like them against the world. Layered on top of that, the brotherhood of homicide cops was even more closely forged.

Between them on the gracious coffee table was the plain, government issue manila envelope Copeland had dumped there, containing documentation which should never had reason to exist, carrying an innocuous, typed label. How many such envelopes had these men shared? How many had it taken to impress on them the baseness of human nature, the depths that man was capable of sinking to? How many to sculpt the resigned expressions on their faces and eyes that their smiles never reached, the weight of their being?

This was not the first time the two men had been through the contents of the envelope. They looked again through the photographs of the dead victim, at the pathologist's report. She had died from a skull fracture and consequent haemorrhage. No trace materials of relevance from the corpse. No signs of a struggle. A photo of the space in the kitchenette where she had been killed. The blood stain on the tiles. Spatter on the edge of the carpet in the adjoining living room. The murder weapon. The wine glass containing the two sets of fingerprints, one set cupping the glass, the other around the middle. A report identifying the owners of the prints. No telling phone calls from the victim or suspects. None on the night of the murder.

"So, what have we got and what are we missing?" asks Morrison. "Who and why?"

"Well, whoever it was, she knew them. We know that. Not some druggie off the street. Was it a spur of the moment thing? Or a premeditated crime?"

"Can't know for sure. If it was planned ahead, the killer knew the murder weapon would be there. He or she had been there before. Or they could have just lost it and grabbed the bookend."

"We have a 'she' here too. Barnwell's wife. Jealousy and the threat to her marriage as a motive."

"But no knowledge of her husband's infidelity. As far as we can ascertain. Same with Brookes' missus. No sign of her knowing what good, old, upstanding Howard was up to."

"We're a fine species. It's a wonder, mate, that you and I have any faith in human nature left," said Copeland.

"The scary part, mate, is that you're the one that gives me my faith in humankind," answered Morrison.

"Aw shucks."

"You and your law degree. You could be making a lot more money out there as a defence lawyer keeping the bastards out of jail. But you know as well as I do, that you stayed in this shit business so you can get them put away, keep them off the streets."

"Yeah, well, I'm not the only one. There's a whole bunch of us mad bastards driven by that sweet thought. And that includes you too. Although I suppose we *are* a select few when you look at the big picture."

"What does that say about you and me? Most people avoid death like the plague. But we're drawn to it. It's the people who *do* these things that repel us. Someone has to deliver justice to the victims and prevent further violence. Whether that means we are not *normal,* I'm not sure. We're probably not. But I don't know how we won the prize."

"As far as Rachel Klein's killer goes, we keep coming back to Barnwell. Motive, no alibi, the fingerprints on the glass. You know, mate, 'Occam's razor'. The simplest explanation is most likely the correct one."

"But, upstanding member of the community. Good family. Good school. No criminal record. Not even a traffic violation. No history of violence."

"It happens. Doesn't fit the usual profile of a killer. But intelligent people with normal upbringings have murdered when the motive was there. Just look at our home-grown killer, Baden-Clay."

"That wasn't a happy home though. The wife was showing signs of abuse."

"Yeah well, how happy were the Barnwells if he was off having an affair though?"

"We haven't proof of the affair. Only the say-so of Klein's friend. According to Barnwell, the time spent at her place was all work related."

"Right. And we believe that?"

"Yeah. Pigs might fly. Don't think a jury would swallow it either."

"Not many calls made to each other, according to their records. And any that were made can be explained away as work related too."

"What about him attacking her from behind? She had dropped him, started up with Brookes. Vincent felt emasculated because she had moved up to someone with more power and prestige than he, Barnwell, had. He felt rejected. He was jealous, angry. He had been extremely invested in her. Wouldn't he have wanted her to see it coming, see the satisfaction on his face?" asked Copeland.

"We might need a forensic psychologist for that one. Some of them reckon when the killer feels he's being 'stabbed in the back', then he attacks from the back. Who knows? But it might have been purely practical. He didn't want to risk her fighting back, defensive wounds, his DNA under her fingernails. Remember how incriminating the scratch on Baden-Clay's face was? He told a doctor he did it shaving. Blind Freddie could tell it was made by fingernails."

"Want another coffee?"

"Thanks. I could do with something stronger but we're still on work time."

"Yeah, even though we'll still be going at nine tonight."

"Have we ruled out Brookes altogether? I mean, his fingerprints were on the glass too. And he has admitted to screwing her. But he has an alibi. No motive. No fingerprints anywhere else in the apartment," said Morrison.

"No motive that we know of. She might have been threatening to tell the wife. And prints aren't always left. They like glass because it's non-porous."

"Klein doesn't seem to be the type to threaten the wife. She was a pretty classy piece, from what I know of her."

"I can't shake the thought that the glass was planted. I don't know. All just too odd with two sets of prints. But there's just no way of knowing how it could have been planted. And both glasses matched sets in Klein's kitchen."

"Well, the brief will go to the DPP. Let them decide whether or not to lay charges.

Let the chips fall where they may.

PART TWO

HOW IT ALL CHANGED

VINCENT

R v Barnwell [2020] QSC 214
Just think, future students of Criminal Law will be able to look up this case reference to read the transcript of my trial in the Queensland Supreme Court before the esteemed Paynter J.

The Accused, Vincent Anthony Barnwell, is charged that on or about 7 December 2019, at Brisbane, he murdered Rachel Helen Klein.
He says he is not guilty.
The role of the jury is to determine, on the evidence, whether he is guilty or not guilty.

I remember the very many times that I, as a law student, went to the Law Library to find the heavy volume with its plain hard binding containing the case we had all been told to read and to pore over.

Now I, Vincent Barnwell, will become a subject for these eager young minds. To say that this feels surreal may sound trite, but that is exactly how it feels. My whole life has become a twilight zone, has been for some time now.

You know, it happens to people. Their life is travelling along more or less as it was meant to, as good as it gets, the usual ups and downs, and then — out of the blue as they say

— the legendary lightning bolt strikes.

Yes — It can happen

The fall from grace was initiated by those chilling words, "I am arresting you on suspicion of murder. I must inform you that you do not have to say or do anything, but anything you say or do may be given in evidence."

So, the nightmare began. Arrest. Questioning (lawyers present). Charge. Fortunately, bail was granted in the Supreme Court. This was, his lawyer argued, because the applicant faced a lengthy period on remand prior to committal proceedings, had no history of violence, was not a flight risk and posed little chance of further offending. Alleged murderers were sometimes granted bail these days, when there were 'exceptional circumstances'. Vincent felt that he was back at university studying the Bail Act.

Seven months and a committal hearing later, his trial was beginning tomorrow.

Gillian had not failed him, not for one day. His partnership had, of course, been suspended. It might as well have been terminated. He knew that he would never be returning, whatever the outcome of the trial. The workplace couldn't have been easy for Gillian either, as a criminal lawyer. But she carried on as she always did, with calmness and assurance. She did not doubt him, did not accuse him, did not question him.

She had been, as always, his rock. How he could have risked his life with her, his partnership, his reputation, the peace of mind of his parents, of his brother, and now his very freedom? seemed a question impossible to answer with any degree of reason. The memories of Rachel's charms, of the lust that had consumed him, were fading only too quickly, were out of all perspective to the troubles and fears now overtaking his being.

They had taken a week's holiday away now, the week he hadn't had time for when Gillian wanted it. They tried not to talk about the coming trial, though the thought of it was, of course, never really off their minds. There was a consciousness that they might in the foreseeable future be unable to have weeks like this for a very long time. Somehow, Vincent was never in doubt that if the worst happened, if he went to prison, Gillian would be waiting for him when he came out. Her loyalty was absolute.

Their sex was frantic, desperate, more like the sex he had experienced with Rachel. Perhaps because his time with Gillian now took on the undercurrent of stolen, illicit moments that it had with Rachel. Strange that this aspect of his life was heightened when so much else was so diminished.

They walked along the headland tracks of Noosa National Park, passing the pretty beaches and following the smell of eucalyptus and the sound of the whip birds calling, until they reached the Boiling Pot. There they watched as the waves fizzed across the rocks, and searched the treetops for koalas snoozing in the branches and for black cockatoos. They continued on to Dolphin Point and looked out over the ocean, hoping to see a pod of dolphins or maybe a sea turtle. Locals said that in season (June to November) whales could be heard singing beneath the waves. The crowning point was possibly the morbid sounding Hell's Gate, a sandstone cave carved out by the pounding surf.

They like to dine at Sails, with its Laguna Bay vista and its fusion menu featuring local seafoods, together with a wide selection of Australian, New Zealand and European wines. Gillian, in particular, seemed to like browsing in the boutique shops and art galleries of Hastings Street. The 'Noosa Psychic Clairvoyant Reading with Linda' sign attracted Vincent's attention, though it never had before. He shook the thought off.

How wonderful his life had been, before Rachel. What would life be like in a year's time?

At home they talked about the trial. Gillian was unfailingly reassuring. He had told her that he had not had an affair with Rachel. He doubted that she believed him, but she never said so. Could she really believe that he had gone to Rachel's place to work? He had had to tell her that he had been there; it would certainly come up in court. The police had asked him about the fingerprints. He could only say that they must have been left on the glass months ago, the glass put away before being properly washed. The prints puzzled him too. His mind turned to them again and again. Gillian, of course, knew about Howard's fingerprints, though he did not. She felt that, as she had planned, they would confuse a jury enough for him to be let off.

Vincent's feelings were in a constant turmoil. Uppermost was fear. Fear, he remembered, engenders a fight or flight reaction in us. For him, there was no possibility of flight. His only option was to fight, fight within the adversarial arena known as our justice system. But he knew as well as any, that the fight did not always deliver justice. It was an imperfect system. The courtroom was a place where sometimes good things happened to good people and bad things happened to bad people. But there was an element of chance, and at times, bad things happened to good people. Truth did not always equate to justice. Vincent was only too aware of that. He was, after all, married to a criminal lawyer. Being only too aware of what happened in courtrooms, therefore, did little to allay his fear.

He also felt alternating feelings of anger, self-pity and paranoia. But there was always an undercurrent of just wanting his old life back. He wanted things to be as they were before he had allowed himself to be drawn in to the thrall of Rachel, before he had been reduced from upstanding citizen to a position so low on the social ladder, that it was nigh impossible to fall any further.

Visits from friends were only occasional and so awkward that Vincent was glad when they left. Of course, they knew that this was a terrible miscarriage of justice. They knew what kind of person he was. They were behind him all the way. Vincent knew that this was not entirely true. No matter how long people had known him, they had had their doubts. As per usual, the general public had already found him guilty. Once charged you were guilty. The 'Letters to the Editor' section were full of calls for him to be locked up for life. There were calls to bring back the death penalty. He was — privileged, private school, wealthy, entitled, thought he was above the law. He would probably get special treatment in the courts because he was a lawyer, his family were lawyers. They all stuck together, people said. One law for the poor and another for the rich. There was little mention of the basic tenet that you were innocent until proven guilty.

But perhaps the sadness in the eyes of his parents was the thing that hurt Vincent the most. Of course, they were unconditionally supportive. But he knew that their lives were now over. And what the publicity was doing to his brother and his children, he could only imagine.

The press were in a frenzy.

LAWYER CHARGED WITH LOVER'S MURDER

A prominent lawyer has been charged with the murder of his paralegal in Brisbane's inner city.

The police have been investigating the death of twenty-four-year-old Rachel Klein who was found dead in her apartment by her cleaner, in Fortitude Valley, two kilometres north of Brisbane's CBD, on the morning of 8th October last year.

Officers attended and found the body of the woman, who had been brutally bashed.

Vincent Barnwell has been charged with her murder.

A source close to the victim has revealed that Barnwell had been involved in an extramarital affair with Klein. It appears that Klein had ended the affair.

Barnwell's wife, a Brisbane criminal lawyer, declined to comment.

Now the day had finally come. Tomorrow, his trial was to begin in the Brisbane Supreme Court before the formidable Justice Paynter. Vincent was sitting in the office of his lawyer poring over the state's evidence as revealed in the discovery process which ensures that the accused person is properly informed of the case against him. In accordance with the Queensland Criminal Code, it is a fundamental obligation of the prosecution to ensure that the proceedings operate fairly, with the single aim of determining and establishing the truth. In Australia, the requirement extends to material that is averse to the prosecution's case.

Vincent wished that a trial *did* always establish the truth. But from what he knew, only too well, of the criminal justice system, that was by no means always the case.

So my lawyers and I come to the case against me. There are reports, transcripts of interviews. There are witnesses. Senior Constable Malcolm Chalmers can describe the scene of the crime as it was first discovered. Detective Inspector Lindsay Copeland could attest to my having admitted to being at the home of the victim, on several occasions. Rachel Klein's friend would be called to say that Rachel had told her of having been personally involved with me (this would be hearsay, my lawyer assures me, to be disregarded).

The worrying piece of evidence, the only physical evidence, is the wine glass with my prints on it. However, what startles us, what renders us momentarily mute, is that the very same glass also carries the fingerprints of the upstanding, decorous, Mr Howard Brookes.

My mind is hardly able to grasp this new information. Rachel and Howard. Had he known about me? I had been working with both of them, seeing them almost every day. Wouldn't I have noticed, well, something? And in all these months of awaiting trial, Howard had not seen fit to tell me.

But finally, there was the beginning of hope.

What we leave behind.

VINCENT

Maurice Rafferty QC, Chief Crown Prosecutor, opened for the Crown. He was big and bluff, a likeable-looking man with an open face inspiring trust, his figure massive in his black gown, wig squarely on his large, squarish head.

He had the rapt attention of every person in the courtroom. The jury filled the box, their faces solemn and intent on every word that was spoken.

Justice Paynter, a grey-haired, stern-looking man, presided. His eyes were piercing eyes, that seemed to reach into every nook and cranny he surveyed. None would dare test him.

Formalities over, opening statements began.

"Members of the jury,

On the evening of 7th of October 2019, a beautiful, promising young woman had her life abruptly and violently taken from her.

Rachel Klein cannot be with us today.

The man accused of her murder can.

That man is the defendant, Vincent Barnwell, who is right here in this courtroom this morning.

It is your duty, the most solemn of civic duties, to listen to the evidence, to weigh that evidence, deliberate upon it, determine what actually occurred.

You will hear that the accused is an upstanding member

of the community, a man of the law whose character has never before been in question. This is not disputed.

Upstanding members of the community *have* been shown to have committed violent crimes before today.

You will also hear that the defendant worked closely with the victim. You will find that his relationship with her went beyond the workplace, that he was, on several occasions, welcomed into her home. A close friend of the deceased will throw further light on the nature of her relationship with the accused.

Your job will be to reach a reasonable conclusion as to the nature of that relationship and where it stood at the time of the victim's death.

You will hear that the defendant purports to have been at his home on the night of the victim's death. You will be asked to decide whether that can indeed be established on the facts.

You will hear that the accused's familiarity with the deceased's home will have made him aware of the presence there of the murder weapon.

You will be presented with physical evidence showing that the defendant was present in the victim's home on the evening of her murder.

You will be asked to reach a conclusion as to the presence of motive and opportunity on the part of the accused.

A crime has been committed. The crime is murder.

It is your sworn duty to weigh the evidence presented in this courtroom and decide whether the accused is guilty of this most serious of crimes."

Vincent sat and listened, feeling as though this were happening to someone else and not him. Everyone in the courtroom but him still had some dignity in their lives, the respect of peers, some degree of happiness or the ability to seek it. Now he was a pariah, accused, soon to be judged, for the most heinous of crimes. And he was helpless to do anything about it. He could simply sit and wait, with only a vestige of hope to cling to.

Roland Burns QC, now had his turn. He was a compact man, well presented, Maurice Rafferty's opposite in many ways, neat in his robe, serious and reflective as he addressed the jury.

"A young man sits before you today. He is a man of character, of unblemished reputation, respected by all who know him.

"Today you hold the freedom of this man in your hands. You will hear evidence. You will be asked to weigh this evidence, deliberate upon it. You will be asked to decide on your verdict on the basis of this evidence.

"Foremost in your mind throughout all of the evidence, must be two things. The first is the very basis of the law of this land. That is the *presumption of the innocence*, the line that law draws around every person accused of a crime, a line that no jury may cross until they have been convinced of the second of these things, that it has been showed *beyond reasonable doubt*, that it is this person before you who is the guilty party.
"Until guilt has been proved beyond reasonable doubt, you, the members of jury, may not breach that barrier and take away the precious freedom of the good man before you.

Beyond reasonable doubt.

"You will be asked to listen to much evidence that is circumstantial. Circumstantial evidence attempts to build a chain. That chain is made up of motive, means and opportunity. *Every* link of the chain, members of jury, must be proven to you beyond reasonable doubt. If you have a reasonable doubt about *any* link, the chain is broken, and the chain is unable to tie the defendant here to the body of the victim.

"Any reasonable doubt, about any link, must cause you to reach a verdict of 'not guilty'.

"In this circumstantial case, you will hear not facts, but rather, speculation upon speculation.

"The prosecution's case rests upon the nature of the relationship between Mr Barnwell and Ms Klein. You have heard that they were colleagues who worked closely together. The prosecution will attempt to show that they were also lovers. They need to do this in order to prove motive for the crime. All that they will be able to offer you in this attempt however, is circumstantial evidence. They will *not* be able to prove such a relationship beyond reasonable doubt.

"The only single piece of forensic evidence will also prove nothing that can connect the defendant to the crime beyond reasonable doubt.

"You will, members of the jury, find weak links in the supposed chain.

"You will reach the only the possible verdict."

The first witness for this prosecution, Senior Constable Malcom Chalmers, was called to the stand. He stood before the jury to be sworn.

Rafferty asked first about the crime scene.

"Constable Chalmers, I have here a copy of your report. You were the first responder at the scene, I take it. Is that correct?"

"Yes, that is correct."

Chalmers commanded respect. He was a tall and brown-haired man, with clear blue eyes and an openness and directness. He spoke clearly and with confidence.

"Can you describe for the court what you encountered at the scene?"

"The body of the woman was face down on the floor in a pool of blood," said Chalmers. "This was on the floor of the kitchenette. A bloody object which appeared to be a stone or marble bookend was lying on the floor also."

"Can you tell the court when this was, Constable Chalmers?" asked Rafferty.

"We were called to the scene at around nine o'clock on the morning of 8th October. Her cleaning lady reported her death when she arrived at the victim's apartment at around eight forty-five that morning."

Chalmers told the court of the procedures that followed, the collection of physical evidence by the forensic team, photographs taken, the securing of the scene.

Photographs admitted by the judge were passed among the jurors. Their faces remained passive, not exhibiting the usual abhorrence observed in such Hollywood movie scenes.

However, the prosecution's intent was always to create an aversion in the jurors to the unfortunate person accused of the crime, and he had no choice but to sit helpless and silent, no matter what transpired.

"Was there any sign of the apartment being broken into?"

"No," replied Chalmers. "None at all. It appeared that the perpetrator had been let into the apartment. The cleaning woman found the door locked and had used her own key to enter, as usual."

"Were any windows or doors opened or unlocked?" asked Rafferty.

"No, all windows and the sliding door to the deck were closed."

"Would you conclude that the intruder was someone known to Ms Klein?" asked Rafferty.

"Objection. Your Honour," Burns interrupted, "that calls for speculation."

"Sustained," ruled the judge.

"You described finding two wine glasses on the kitchen bench," continued Rafferty. He picked up photographs among the physical evidence. "These would be the two glasses exhibited here."

"Yes, sir."

"How many types of each wine glass did you find at Ms Klein's home?"

"There were five of the taller one and two of the other in the glass cupboard in the kitchen."

"And that includes the two glasses here?"

"Yes, sir. Six and three in total."

"Thank you, Constable."

"No further questions, Your Honour."

Burns now moved to cross examine.

"Constable Chalmers, you say that the only two doors to the apartment were locked when you arrived. Is that correct?"

"Yes, that is correct."

"And did either of these doors have a deadlock?"

"No, there were no deadlocks."

"Is it possible that one of doors, say the entry door, had been left unlocked by Mrs Klein on the evening of the murder?" asked Burns.

"It is possible, I suppose. But it doesn't seem likely," Chalmers answered.

"But you agree it is possible."

"Yes, Sir."

"And is it possible that the same person could have locked the door on their way out? As you say, it was not deadlocked."

"Yes. Again, it is possible."

"So, it is possible, therefore, that the offender was a person unknown to Mrs Klein. Someone who entered through an unlocked door and was able to lock the door on the way out, as it was a lock that did not require a key. Would you agree that that that was possible?"

"Yes, Sir. It is possible."

"Thank you, Constable."

"No further questions."

Vincent had never felt so isolated. In everything else he had done — law examinations, job interviews, work related matters — there was always someone in the same boat. But here, in this courtroom, there was only one accused facing the obstacle. Him. Vincent Barnwell. Completely alone. The only one who would be found either 'guilty' or 'not guilty'.

And there was no way of hastening the process, of getting to the end, of knowing one way or the other, how it would all finish.

Every detail would be extracted from the witnesses.

The wheels of justice turn slowly but grind exceedingly fine.

VINCENT

Next to be called was Detective Inspector Lindsay Copeland, impressive, calm and intelligent, in command. He was a man who could have aspired to anything, but had chosen to devote his life to seeking justice.

The appearance of total impartiality is the one particular characteristic which has been shown to give weight to a police officer's testimony. Detective Copeland inspired nothing, if not confidence, and gave an air of being professional and dispassionate.

"Detective Inspector Copeland, you are the lead detective on the Rachel Klein murder case. Is that correct?" asked Rafferty.

"Yes. That is correct." Copeland addressed the jury directly. They were the most important persons in the room.

"You have stated in your report that you have interviewed the defendant on four separate occasions. Could you confirm that for the court?"

"Yes, that is so."

The jury listened, intently. This witness, the lead detective, would surely provide them with vital answers. The photographs of Rachel Klein's battered body were still at the forefront of their mind. It was difficult for some of them not to feel some revulsion toward the defendant, even if rationally they knew the unjustness of that. They looked to this man on the stand for his professional opinion, for those very insights which would allow them to bring down a verdict.

The press was, of course, there in force. They had taken their photos of Vincent and Gillian as they walked, faces impassive, up the steps of the courtroom on the first morning of the trial.

Then there was Vincent's family. Gillian was seated with his parents and his brother. Gillian was, as usual, wonderful. She was wearing a navy, linen shift with a simple, silver chain and earrings and plain, black pumps. Her exquisite face with its unfathomable, pale-grey eyes which seemed, as always, to conceal a well of mystery, betrayed nothing of her feelings. Next to her, Vincent's parents appeared suddenly old and tired and weighed down. The sadness in their eyes was inescapable. His brother seemed to be their only strength. He sat on the other side of them, erect, stoic, solemn. Gillian's good friend, Hilary, was there as support but did not sit with the family. Ann was there as well. Gillian had at least two good friends.

Gillian's parents had been unable to face the courtroom.

Rafferty continued, congenial and courteous, yet somehow formidable. He established that Barnwell and Klein had had a close working relationship, that sometimes necessitated continuing into the evening.

"And was their working back late confined to their office at the legal partnership where they worked?"

"No, not on every occasion."

"Did Mr Barnwell say where else he and Ms Klein would continue this after-hours work?"

"Yes, he said that sometimes they would go to Ms Klein's apartment."

"Did he say on how many occasions this occurred?" asked

Rafferty.

"Yes, he said that they went to the apartment on four separate occasions," answered Copeland.

"And this was for the purpose of continuing legal work after hours?"

"Yes. That is so."

"Did Mr Barnwell and Ms Klein ever adjourn to Barnwell's home for the purpose of continuing their work after hours?"

"No. They did not."

"Did the defendant explain why not?"

"Yes. Mr Barnwell said it was easier at Ms Klein's apartment as no one else was there. In other words, there were no distractions. At his home, his wife would probably there."

"Did the defendant explain why he preferred to continue after hours work at Ms Klein's apartment rather than in the workplace?" Rafferty continued.

"He said that it was — I believe his word was — 'nicer' to be able to spread out in the living room," said Copeland.

"Did this arrangement strike you as unusual?"

"Objection. This calls for the speculation," interjected Burns.

"Sustained. Please move on, Mr Rafferty." From the judge.

"Yes, Your Honour. Detective, did the defendant say how long it had been since he had last been at the home of deceased?"

"He said it had been about two months."

"Did Mr Barnwell say why there had been such a long period of not working back?" asked Rafferty.

"Yes. He said that he had not had need for Ms Klein's input during that time," Copeland answered.

"In such a very busy legal practice?"

"That is what Mr Barnwell said."

"And could the defendant account for his whereabouts on the night of the murder?"

"He said that he was at home all evening."

"Did he not leave his home at any point?"

"Mr Barnwell said he had not."

"Is there anyone who can vouch for that?"

"No, he was alone. His wife had stayed back at work 'til about a quarter to eight.

Burns cross examined.

"Detective Inspector, did you question the defendant as to the nature of his relationship with the victim?"

"Yes, sir."

"And how did Mr Barnwell describe the relationship?"

"He described it as purely professional."

"And did the defendant give you any reason to doubt the assertion?"

"No, he did not."

"Thank you, Detective Inspector," said Burns.

"Turning your attention to the night Ms Klein died, Detective. Mr Barnwell asserts that he was home all evening. Did you check location history for that night?"

"Yes, we did."

"And what did you find?"

"Location history showed that the defendant was at home for the stated period of time."

"The Barnwell's, I believe, possess only one car. Is that correct?"

"That is my understanding."

"And on the particular night in question, according to your

report, their one car had been in the carport at his wife's law firm?" Burns asked.

"Yes, that is correct," answered Copeland.

"How were you able to establish that fact?"

"Footage from the CCTV showed their car parked in that carpark and also showed Mrs Barnwell leaving the carpark at around 7.45 p.m."

"So, it seems that the defendant did not have access to a car on the night of the murder."

"That seems to be the case."

"You established with TransLink that the defendant travelled by bus, using his Go-card, from the stop near his workplace to the stop nearest his home, arriving at about 6.15 p.m. Do I understand that correctly?" asked Burns.

"Yes, that it what the report says."

"And his wife phoned him from her car at around 7.45 p.m. when he must have been at home to answer her call. Did the location finder establish that?"

"Yes, that was established."

"You have established from the records that such a call was made and received?"

"Yes, that has been established."

"Did you check with all taxi and ride-share companies as to whether a fare had been taken to the address of the victim between 6.15 and 8 p.m.?"

"Yes, we checked with all the companies."

"And what did you find?" asked Burns.

"There were no records of any such fare at any company."

"Thank you, Detective. Would you agree that it is hardly feasible that the defendant travelled by public transport, in other words by bus, to the home of Ms Klein, committed the crime, and then travelled home again all before his wife phoned arrived home at around 8 p.m.?"

"I agree that it is hardly feasible, but it is just possible. We have checked bus timetables," said Copeland.

"But you would agree barely feasible," asked Burns, "taking into account the possibility of just missing a bus at any juncture."

"Yes, I would have to agree with that."

On redirect, the prosecution pointed out that the location history merely established that the accused's mobile phone was at his home. In other words, Vincent may have gone out but not taken his phone with him. A small victory perhaps, but there remained in the jurors' minds, the almost impossible to believe scenario, of a killer catching a bus in order to murder someone.

Gillian, her criminal law mind at work, knew that reasonable doubt had been established as to whether Vincent could possibly have made it to Rachel's home in the time available. No motive had been established yet either. She had asked Vincent about what was contained in the brief of evidence. He had not found the courage to bring up Michelle Hildebrande's statement about Rachel telling her of her affair with him, and that she had broken it off. He was sure that in court this would be ruled out as hearsay, before it even got off the ground. At least he hoped so. Who knew what a judge might rule! Would he decide that the victim should be allowed a voice from beyond the grave? But surely not. God, how he hated that bitch Rachel now. How could he ever have been besotted with her!

Gillian knew it did not sound good that Vincent had worked with Rachel at her home. But while that possibly suggested a personal relationship, without evidence, that was it all it amounted to - suggestion. And the clincher was still to come - the second set of fingerprints.

It was going well; they would have to acquit. Gillian had hoped that it would not have made it as far as trial. But now that it had, everything was falling into place, thanks to her careful planning.

Allegations, all just allegations.

VINCENT

The testimony of the state's forensic pathologist, Dr Sondra Burke — small, humble, bespectacled — contained no surprises as to cause of death, but images would have been revived in every mind of every juror of a young, beautiful woman who had crumpled to the floor, then lain in a pool of her own blood, her golden hair matted red. They would have pictured once again the base of the heavy bookend, identified as the murder weapon, impacting extremely heavily on the back of the lovely head. Then the photos of this young woman lying face down, alone and untended 'til discovered by the unfortunate cleaner the next morning, would have come back into their minds, if they had ever left.

The jury would have thought of a young life, so promising, no longer to be lived, of those who loved her left behind, of the children who would now never be born.

Did they give the shadowy, missing figure a face? Was it the satisfied face of Vincent Barnwell? Vincent saw them glancing at him, involuntarily it seemed, during the testimony. To what degree did the verdicts of juries, hinge on emotions, and how much on fact?

Rachel Klein's parents, Stan and Helen, sat rigid, silent tears wetting their cheeks. The whole court room was still, taking in the horrific details, picturing the scene. Vincent felt the eyes on him, people wondering if this man sitting so alone could be a capable of this. Some wept without sound. Others sobbed, the muffled gasps the only outward signs of the conflicting emotions gripping the solemn room.

At last, the morning session was over, and the adjournment for lunch declared by the judge.

Lunch was sandwiches and coffee delivered to a small, windowless room in the multistorey building. It was just Vincent, Gillian and Roland Burns. Vincent's parents had decided to go out for fresh air. Perhaps, Vincent thought, they could not take any more of this. Perhaps they wanted to console each other. What would they truly be thinking of his after-hours assignations with Rachel? Outwardly, they would not express any doubts or disappointment with him, but would they really believe that there had been no intimacy? Thinking about them was possibly the hardest part of all of this. They had always been so proud of him.

Roland was wanting to look forward, to think about what the rest of the prosecution case would look like. The fingerprint expert would be vital for the prosecution case. Fingerprints were fact, as far as juries were concerned. The case would move out of the merely circumstantial to hard, physical evidence. There would be a glass with Vincent's fingerprints on it, a glass that was found in the victim's home on the morning after the murder, only a short distance from the body. Of course, there were also Brookes' fingerprints on the same glass, which should hopefully confuse the jury enough to establish reasonable doubt. The defence would use the argument that the prints had been left at an earlier date.

Then there would be Hildebrande, repeating what Rachel had said about the affair and the ending of it. Roland and Gillian, expected that this would be disregarded as hearsay.

The state would be hoping for her testimony to be allowed. So far, any attempt they had made to establish motive had been weak, and they would be wanting to plant the suggestion of jealousy and rejection. This was a common motive among male killers.

The state's case, in a nutshell, was that Vincent and Rachel had been having an affair. He had become obsessed with her. She had ended the relationship and moved on to someone more attractive to her. Vincent knew about the other man. He had been unable to accept her rejection and his jealousy and despair reached the point, where he could deal with this only by murdering the woman he was obsessed with, as so many men before him had done.

Their case was largely circumstantial. The only physical evidence would be the fingerprints on the glass.

There remained the question of whether Gillian should take the stand.

The prosecution had decided not to call her. Gillian knew only too well that she could be subpoenaed. It was a common myth that a wife could not be made to testify against their husband. They could, however, object if there was likely to be harm caused to their relationship with the defendant, unless the harm caused was outweighed by the desirability of having the court hear the evidence. This would be up to the judge. The nature and gravity of the offence would be a major factor. If subpoenaed in this case, a murder trial, Gillian would almost certainly have to take the stand.

The prosecution must have decided, therefore, that her testimony would not necessarily act in their favour.

So, should the defence call Gillian? Vincent did not voice the seemingly obligatory objection to his wife's taking the stand, as was the usual stance taken by husbands in television crime dramas. This was real-life drama. If Gillian's appearance would help his case, then he wanted his wife as a witness.

All Burns would want of her was to reassure the jury that their marriage was solid and happy, and that she was in no doubt that her husband's relationship with Rachel Klein had been simply a professional one. He would hope to counter the suggestions to the contrary that Rafferty had attempted.

But what would the prosecution do with her on cross? How would they suggest to the jury that Vincent might have been experiencing discontent, to suggest that Vincent might not be as happy in his marriage as the veneer appeared?

One way that presented itself to Burns would be to elicit from Gillian her higher status and earnings, as senior partner, compared to Vincent's. Add to this her higher qualifications, a Masters of Law, with a hint that all of this might erode a normal, red-blooded man's ego and drive him into the arms of a woman where he was in the power position.

"Roland, surely not," said Gillian. "That's outrageous. So sexist. You would object. No judge would allow that line of questioning."

"No, no judge would allow it. I would immediately object on the grounds of relevance. If Rafferty proceeded, he would be asking to speculate on a matter directly outside of your field of knowledge. But on top of that, it would be beyond the bounds of propriety. The problem is, by the time the judge ruled, the seed would have been planted as far as the jury goes, and there are seven men on the jury."

"That's always the problem," replied Gillian, "but I would have thought that a man like Rafferty would be embarrassed to imply something like that," said Gillian.

"Who knows? But I'm raising possibilities. But on top of that he would most certainly ask you if you knew about Vincent's work sessions at Klein's home. You have told the police that you did not. Rafferty would suggest that that was unusual," said Burns.

"I would emphasise that Vincent and I are not each other's keepers. We are busy professionals who respect each other's space and do not expect to be informed of every detail of the other's working arrangements."

"That may not be the attitude of the ordinary person, male or female. It might not sit well. My view is that it may be best not to put you on the stand."

"I don't know," replied Gillian. "Seeing his wife being so supportive of him could be very reassuring to the jury. That's almost certainly why the prosecution did not call me."

They didn't make a decision at that point, but left it to think about further.

Vincent would not be taking the stand. While juries might want to hear the accused say he was innocent, there were some questions that the prosecution may ask that Vincent might not want to answer truthfully. Was that why Roland himself had not asked him directly whether he had killed Rachel? He did not want Vincent on the stand if he was not going to tell the whole truth. For the jury to sense that would be a disaster.

Neither man looked at Gillian during this exchange, and Gillian remained silent.

Following lunch, a finger print expert, Audrey Chung, gave testimony. She began with a simple explanation of fingerprint basics, emphasising the uniqueness of each fingerprint. It scarcely seemed necessary. Everyone, it seems, has seen forensics at work on at least one of the many crime shows on offer on television. Everyone has watched a fictional murderer donning gloves or wiping surfaces or objects clean of their prints.

Ms Chung was then asked about the two wine glasses found on Klein's kitchen bench on the morning that the body had been found. The first had the prints of only Rachel Klein on it. It matched two others found in her glasses' cupboard in the kitchenette.

"And the second glass, also exhibited here," asked Rafferty. "Did it contain the fingerprints, Ms Chung, of the defendant, Mr Vincent Barnwell?"

"Yes. Yes, it did. It had the defendant's fingerprints on it. Those on the glass matched those voluntarily submitted to the police by Mr Barnwell."

A murmur ran through the courtroom. Jury members could not resist glancing again at the man accused of the murder. Fingerprints didn't lie.

Gillian could sense the 'defendant guilty' mood of the courtroom. She, however, could hardly wait for the fly in the ointment that was coming.

Gratification arrived for her on cross examination.

"Ms Chung, you have testified that the fingerprints of the accused were on the so called second glass?" asked Burns.

"Yes, sir. That is correct."

"That is not the end of the matter though, as I understand it. Can you tell the court whether the fingerprints of any other person were detected on the same glass?"

"Yes, fingerprint technology did reveal that a second person had handled that same glass," Ms Chung answered.

"Please don't keep the court in suspense, Ms Chung. Are you able to reveal the identity of this other person?"

"Yes, I am. He had also voluntarily submitted to the police printing. The prints were identified as belonging to a Mr Howard Brookes."

The courtroom broke into a hubbub. The confusion that this revelation had produced was palpable.

The judge called for order.

"And tell the court, Ms Chung, please, were any further prints found on this glass? Those of a third or even a fourth person, perhaps?"

"Only those of Mr Barnwell and Mr Brookes."

"Can you explain, for the court, what length of time it is possible for fingerprints to last on a glass surface?"

"On non-porous surfaces, prints can last a very long time. We have, in fact, no idea how long they can last on a clean, smooth surface that was left untouched. Most fingerprints are from a sweat and oil mixture or skin oils which are non-volatile, and can last a very long time."

"Is it possible that contact with the glass in question could have been made by Mr Barnwell, at a date earlier than the night of the murder?"

"Certainly, that could be the case. It is impossible to arrive at safe conclusions as to when a trace was formed," Ms Chung replied.

"Would washing in water remove the prints from the glass?"

"Not necessarily. Not at all. A greasy print on a piece of glass, for example, may survive months under water. Prints containing oil secretions, which are hydrophobic, are still preserved after getting wet."

"Is it possible then that the accused, Mr Barnwell, left these fingerprints you have identified on this second glass, as we are calling it, a period of a month or more before the death of Ms Klein?"

"Yes, that is indeed possible."

"So the glass could have been subjected to a cursory wash or rinse in water, left to dry on the drainer, and then put away, still retaining the fingerprints of Mr Barnwell?"

"Yes, that is so. That is one possibility, certainly."

"Would detergent added to the water have destroyed these prints?"

"Again, not necessarily. Not without vigorous rubbing. Just a dip and rinse would probably not be sufficient to remove prints."

"In your opinion, could these prints, those of the defendant, have been deposited on the glass in question, say two months prior to the death of the victim, and then those of Mr Brookes added to the same glass, on or about the night of the murder?" Burns asked.

"Objection. Mr Brookes is not on trial here." Rafferty protested.

"Sustained. Mr Burns, you should know better," agreed Judge Paynter.

"Yes, Your Honour. I apologise. Mr Brookes, indeed, is not on trial."

"Mr Burns, I warn you again," said the judge. "You will move on."

"No further questions, Your Honour."

"You may step down, Ms Chung."

Gillian was delighted. All had gone just as she planned. And Howard Brookes deserved the slur on his good name. He alone was responsible for any damage to his reputation. He had rejected his wife of many years, the woman who had always stood by him, raised his children, managed the whole domestic scene so that he could focus solely on his career. He was only getting what he was due.

Vincent remained puzzled about two sets of fingerprints on the glass. He had had a couple of wines at Rachel's, yes. He had noticed now, from courtroom exhibits, that her wineglasses were pretty much the same as ones he and Gillian had at home. Well, he supposed they were a popular modern style and naturally would be common in many households. Most wine glasses looked much the same. He shrugged off these thoughts. What did it matter? The glass must have given the jury cause for reasonable doubt. He felt sweet relief.

Ann was in the courtroom. Gillian saw her standing and leaving, holding her head high, as soon as the fingerprint evidence was over. Gillian would have loved to have followed her, but wanted to hear Michelle Hildebrand's testimony. She would phone Ann to see if they could get together mid-afternoon. She needed some time with Hilary too. It occurred to her, her only real friends were women who had been rejected by their husbands. She had never really felt a need for friends, but she responded emotionally to a woman's rejection.

But Michelle Hildebrand was taking the stand. Gillian was surprised. She was not what she had expected in Rachel Klein's best friend. Rachel had always looked chic and svelte in pencil skirts and heels, hair well cut and groomed, makeup subtle but expertly applied. Michelle recalled the famous opening lines of George Eliot's *Middlemarch* — having 'that kind of beauty which seems to be thrown into relief by poor dress'. She *was* beautiful but in a way that seemed to disdain

Rachel's evident vanity. Her bone structure and wide eyes needed little makeup. She was dressed in earthy boho style, slouchy sundress, embroidered jacket, wooden beads around her throat and flat, brown, ankle boots on her feet. It was certainly not the usual courtroom attire. Her long, ash blond hair was scraped back into a loose knot. When she was sworn in, her voice was clear and somehow sensuous. Her gaze took in the whole courtroom and she appeared poised and self-assured but at the same time, unpretentious. What was it that she and Rachel had shared?

You wear it well.

"Ms Hildebrand, how long had you and Ms Klein known each other?" asked Rafferty.

"We met when we were at primary school, year five, I think," answered Michelle. "Rachel was my best friend. We met for drinks every Friday after work. We were very close. We supported each other through everything. I miss her every day of my life," Michelle answered.

"I suppose the court can take it that you and she shared confidences, told each other your deepest, darkest secrets, as they say."

"We did. We trusted each other implicitly. You could say that we told each other everything."

"That is what I will be asking you about today," said Rafferty. "I will be asking you about some of those confidences. I understand this is difficult for you but it is all part of making sure of the fairness of this trial and of the verdict. We are all here in the pursuit of justice."

"Mr Rafferty. Sir. Your Honour." The witness turned to look at Justice Paynter. She stood silent but did not lower her eyes. She waited a moment.

"Ms Hildebrand?" queried Rafferty.

"I just can't do this. I know it's the right thing to do. But it's not right by Rachel. It's just not right. The things she told me *were* in confidence. She didn't expect me to repeat them to anybody, much less the whole world. I'm sorry for wasting your time."

"I'm sorry, Ms Hildebrand," Justice Paynter intervened, "but I'm afraid you don't have a choice in the matter. You have been called upon to testify and you are obliged to answer all questions put to you. I believe the police have your signed witness statement. However, the jury is entitled to hear from you in person. I have to warn you that to refuse to answer questions here will put you in contempt of court." The judge left no room for doubt. "I have decided to adjourn until tomorrow morning. Mr Rafferty, I suggest that you speak seriously to your witness in the meantime."

Words left unsaid

ANN

Ann was pleased to have the opportunity to meet with Gillian for coffee, mid-afternoon. She was desperate to have someone to talk the events of the morning over with, and Gillian was the only person she could think of.

"Oh, that was just awful in the court this morning Gillian," said Ann.

"I know it was. It's just horrible, isn't it? Having these insinuations made publicly. It's like having the whole world watching and making up their minds about you."

"Yes, all that about the fingerprints. Everybody will be so sure that Howard and that bitch Rachel were involved. Everybody will be gossiping about it, thinking of me as some kind of castoff. It's all so embarrassing. And the kids! Oh, my god. The kids!"

"I know Ann. It's a dreadful time for you. Have you spoken to Howard?" Gillian asked.

"He's been trying to ring, but I just can't bring myself to answer at the moment. Of course, he will have heard what happened in court, and imagine the headlines in tomorrow morning's papers. They won't be able to get enough of it."

"Yes, I know only too well what it's like. We've endured enough of those ugly headlines. Tomorrow it will just get uglier. It's a nightmare," said Gillian.

"Gillian, I'm so sorry. I'm going on and on about myself.

You're the one whose husband's going through this dreadful trial. I can't even imagine what it's like for you. And for Vincent. As if he would be capable of such a thing. That Klein woman was a curse. I, for one, am glad she is dead. But her death has unleashed all sorts of horrors. Now they've insinuated in court that Howard might have done it."

"I don't know if it's even proper for us to be meeting, considering what's been going on in the courtroom, but I'm beyond caring," Gillian said. "I suppose the second set of fingerprints establishes reasonable doubt. At least I hope so. But I am sorry that it comes at a cost for you."

Of course, that had been Gillian's plan all along, set in motion when she had retrieved the glass on the night of the dinner party. But Ann would never know that. Your own interests have to come first. That was just human nature.

"Now there's this Hildebrande woman with her confidences," said Ann. "Who knows what that's going to be about."

"If it's just her repeating things Rachel said. It should be disregarded as hearsay," said Gillian. "But you never know what a judge will decide. The prosecution obviously thinks she will be of value. I'm not looking forward to it."

"The kids are supposed to be coming over for dinner tonight. I suppose it'll be best to have this whole thing out. No point putting it off. They're not coming 'til seven, so Howard and I will have time to talk things out. I don't know whether to let him know, that I know about his brief fling with that unspeakable piece of work. Maybe it's better to keep up the pretence. Don't know how to explain his fingerprints being on a glass in her home though. Howard will probably come up with something."

"Ann, I know you want things to just go back to normal for you and Howard, now that Rachel Klein is dead. Will the revelation in court today, and the media storm, mean that won't be possible?"

"Look, that's what's rolling around in my head this afternoon. But I can't see that there's much of a choice. If I break up the marriage, it means a property settlement. My beautiful home would be sold. Our holiday home. I would never have such a lovely home again. Oh, I'd never be poor. But I wouldn't live as well as I do now. And then there's the loneliness."

"You might marry again."

"I can't even imagine. I'd never find another Howard. He *is* a good husband, normally. And now I'd have my uni study as well. Things couldn't get much better apart from this bloody trial of course. The thought of striking out on my own terrifies me."

"I know what you mean. I couldn't imagine life without Vincent either. I just have to remain optimistic about the outcome of the trial. I mean, while they have hinted at a motive, they haven't been able to prove one. And they can't reasonably put Vincent in Rachel Klein's apartment at the time of the death. I think the prosecution's case is starting to fall on its face. So then, we just have to ride out the scandal. That's what you and Howard will have to do too. It'll blow over."

They said their goodbyes, Ann to go home and start making dinner for the family coming over and to discuss the situation with Howard. Gillian would have a quiet night with Vincent and help him relax a little with the trial going so well.

Ann found the house empty. It had been a trying day to say the least but instead of feeling tired, she felt keyed up, adrenaline charged. She found herself listening for Howard's arrival. The sun was going down. There was no daylight saving in Queensland. There were still a couple of hours before the kids arrived. She was sure they would have heard from someone about what had happened in court today but neither of them had phoned. They certainly would have been talking to each other.

Ann felt her nerves getting the better of her — well, what her mother would call 'nerves'. These days, it was 'anxiety'. Her eyes were stinging, and she was having trouble swallowing. She realised her breathing was shallow. She wondered whether she should take a dose of the anti-anxiety medicine prescribed by Dr Matthews. She decided on a Scotch, poured herself one and sat on the sofa to drink it. She poured another. She thought of Howard, and of the kids coming over, and started to feel a buzzing in her head.

She would have to pull herself together, start preparing things for dinner. She began slicing potatoes for the potato bake. It was good to be doing something normal. When Howard came in, she was slicing the eye fillet into thick steaks. When he began talking, she did not look up.

"Ann, what happened in court today. I'm sorry you were there to hear it. You haven't answered any of my calls. You're upset. I understand that," said Howard.

"So you should," answered Ann. "The scandal, the kids. My God."

"Look, these fingerprints on the glass. I can't explain them. I've never been in Rachel Klein's apartment."

"So how did that glass get there?" Ann asked, finishing her slicing, still not meeting her husband's eyes.

"I've had that question rolling round and round in my

head for hours. The only explanation I can come up with is that it was planted."

"By whom?"

"I don't know. Vincent is the only one I can come up with."

"So why would he have left his prints on it? It doesn't make sense."

"He made a mistake? Anyway, the insinuation in court that I might have done it shook me up."

"That was just a play by the defence to get Vincent off. There's no reason, motive or anything, to suspect you."

"Ann, there's something else. Look, you've been the best of wives. A great mother to our kids. I do love you. I will always love you. But it's been hard for me with your battle with depression. I…"

"Hard for you? Really? Hard for you? What about me? All these years of bringing up kids and keeping a perfect home so you could build your career?"

"Well, you've done pretty damned well out of that career. There are a lot of women out there who would have happily swapped places with you."

"Howard, I know about your affair with Rachel Klein. I know about the jewellery. Look, I know what she was like and the effect she had on men. I'm prepared to put it in the past. It's been the only time you've cheated. We can put it behind us. We can get back to normal. We have the kids. Our beautiful home."

"Ann, that's just it. I can't just go on as normal. I just can't. I've experienced something that has changed all that. A passion that we just don't have. I can't live without that now. I have to find that kind of love again. But, it will all be out in the open. I'll pack some things and move out. I really am sorry,

Ann."

In that moment she hated him. She wished him dead. He couldn't do this to her. She couldn't endure it.

Ann picked up the carving knife. She drew it back by her right side, large blade flat, then in one smooth, continuous movement, thrust it into his rib cage. Howard automatically clutched at the site of the pain with both hands. He could not know that his lungs were filling with blood. He was unable even to scream. Astonished, his eyes met those of Ann, cold, impassive, as he slumped to the floor.

You never can tell.

GILLIAN

Gillian answered her phone.

"Gillian. It's Ann. I need you to come over right away. It's urgent."

Ann sounded strange, detached somehow.

"What is it? What's wrong?"

"I've killed Howard. Gillian, Howard's dead."

Gillian paused briefly. That old cliché about feeling as if you were dreaming, well it was right.

"Ann, what did you say? Are you joking?"

Both were stupid questions. She knew exactly what Ann had said. And she knew she wasn't joking.

"Howard's dead, Gillian. I killed him. Look there's no time for this. I need you to come here right now."

"Are you at home?"

"Yes."

"I'm on my way. See you very soon."

Vincent was in the bedroom. She yelled from the living room that she had to go, grabbed her keys and bag and raced to the car. She could see him at the front door, puzzled, watching her as she reversed in a hurry out of their drive and into the street.

Ann had opened the front door by the time Gillian had reached the top of the stairs. Ann led her to the kitchen where she found Howard slumped and twisted, blood coughed from the mouth, the knife still protruding from his abdomen. His face was white. Neither woman had said a word.

Ann spoke first. "He was going to leave me."

"We have to think. Have you rung triple zero?"

"No, I wanted you here."

"Well, phone them now. They'll be able to tell that you rang me first, so we can't undo that. But we don't want to make it any worse." Gillian thought fast. "Quick. Just tell them that your husband is dead and you don't know what happened. Don't say *anything else*. I'll explain later, but do exactly as I say. No, on second thoughts, let me do it."

Gillian took over and spoke to emergency services, going through the drill of name, address, service needed. She gave the minimum of information.

"Ann," Gillian said, "come and sit down now. And listen to me. There is only one way out of this. At the moment, you have to do what I say. The police will be here very soon. Let me do the talking. For the time being, you have just retained me to act as your lawyer. OK? Now I'll be telling them that you first called me as your friend. You were extremely confused. You could not remember what had happened. The last thing you remember is Howard saying that he was the one who killed Rachel, that you had to stand by him, tell no one."

"Gillian, this doesn't make any sense. Why would I say that? How will that help?"

"Just trust me. There is only one defence we can come up with. I'll explain it all when there is time. You *must not*, must not, say that Howard had told you that he was leaving you. That would suggest that you responded in anger. That is the last thing we want. As far as the police are concerned, the last thing you remember is Howard saying that Rachel was blackmailing him over some money laundering thing and that it was he who had killed her. We will not say that you are too upset to speak to the police. That always raises a red flag with them. Ann, tell me that you've got all that."

The knock on the door came soon enough. Gillian opened it to see, not unexpectedly, two grave-faced police officers. They went straight through to the scene, with Gillian in tow.

When they were satisfied and had made phone calls, Gillian showed them to the living room where Ann was still sitting, drained and emotionless.

The police initially recorded Ann's name and address. Gillian explained that she would, for now at least, be acting as Ann's solicitor. They checked with Ann whether that was the case.

Gillian knew that trained investigators would always try to speak to the husband or wife during their time of grief. They know and watch for indicators of whether the grief is real or orchestrated. Who knew what these two would make of Ann, who was not experiencing grief but shock, bewilderment and possibly, a degree of satisfaction?

The paramedics were turned away on arrival. The police turned their attention back to Ann.

"Can you tell us what happened, Ms Brookes?" asked the lead investigator.

"I really don't know. I remember Howard coming home and talking to me. It was awful. I can't remember anything else until I realised Howard was there on the floor. I couldn't wake him," Ann said.

"Do you remember what he was saying to you?" asked the officer.

"He said... oh, my God! He said that he had killed Rachel

Klein. He said she was blackmailing him, because… something about money laundering."

"Officer, I think it is clear that my client is deeply distressed and that there is a period of time here she can't recall. We both know that these procedures have to be humane. I simply can't allow her to answer any further questions at this time. We have to arrange for medical care right away. I'll accompany her as well."

The police officers demurred. It was best to protect themselves. Arrangements were made. The death scene was by now being secured. A forensics team would arrive soon. Then the body would be removed, taken to a funeral director acting for the coroner.

In the hospital room, a doctor spoke to Ann. Ann simply repeated what she had said to the police. The doctor was not there to ascertain any facts for the police. She was not concerned with the alleged crime. She was simply there to benefit Ann's health. She was therefore concerned that there was a period of time of which Ann had no recall. A possibility, of course, was dissociative amnesia. This stemmed from emotional shock or trauma. This could cause the loss of personal and autobiographical information.

On asking Ann relevant questions, however, the doctor found that she could recall perfectly memories of family and social occasions and details about her home, medical history and life story. It was only the specific period of time earlier this evening that was lost to her. She did not appear confused or to have language problems. She was able to answer current affairs questions perfectly well. There was no apparent loss of function. There seemed no reason to order imaging tests to check for brain abnormalities.

It seemed that Ann was already seeing a psychiatrist and intended to continue to do so. All the doctor could do was to see that she was comfortable and treated with gentleness and empathy. She had been through the most terrible experience. The doctor would speak to Ann's nurses.

Gillian was a constant. She, as Ann's lawyer, was permitted to be there. She reassured Ann that they would get through this together. Ann would obviously be arrested and charged with the murder when she was released from hospital. But Gillian was sure she would get off. She would discuss her defence with her when they could have complete privacy.

No one else was permitted to visit, not even Ann's children. A police officer was on watch around the clock.

By the time she was deemed well enough to leave hospital, Gillian had been able to secure bail. Ann met all the conditions, as Vincent had. Gillian took her home to stay with her and Vincent. She could not return to her own cherished home. The worst was yet to come. Ann would have to face her children.

Of course, the events had crucially impacted on Vincent's trial. At 10 a.m. on the morning after Howard's death, Justice Paynter had called both Rafferty and Burns to his chambers. He had had communication from the Director of Public Prosecutions. As the two men had probably heard, Howard Brookes had died on the previous evening. His wife had told police that, just before his death, he confessed to having murdered Rachel Klein.

The trial of Vincent Barnwell was now in a state of disarray. To continue was insupportable.

The lawyers returned to the courtroom.

The judge addressed the court.

"Members of the jury, ladies and gentlemen, information

has come to me last night that urgently and intrinsically affects the very integrity of the trial taking place in this courtroom. It would be improper of me to elaborate any further.

"It is sufficient to say that to continue would amount to abuse of the legal process and condemn the defendant to unjustified distress. I am therefore dismissing this case. Mr Barnwell, you are free to go. I apologise to you unreservedly on behalf of the court.

"Jurors, you are dismissed. I thank you all sincerely."

Twists and turns and headtrips.

ANN

Vincent and Gillian celebrated at their favourite Montrechet as they had not in a very long time. It was all over. Vincent, in particular, was exhilarated. His freedom was guaranteed, his reputation restored, he could still practise his profession. Perhaps the biggest relief of all was that his parents' faith in him would be restored. They would no longer live, in fear. His brother and his wife and their children would no longer be tarnished by his infamy.

The very night was a cliché. No sky had ever been so intoxicating, no stars so alluring, no moon so elusive. Vincent had everything he could wish for. He felt somehow optimistic that it would not be long before they had a child. He was at peace with the world. How could he have ever been so discontent?

You don't know what you've got.

Gillian knew that tomorrow she would have to start to prepare Ann for her trial. Life was so unpredictable. Who could have foreseen that there would be yet another murder trial connected with Rachel Klein? No one could ever know the truth, not even Vincent or Ann's children. She had to keep impressing that on Ann. They had one chance to convince a jury that Ann had suffered a psychological blow that had caused her to kill Howard while in a dissociative state, being disconnected from reality, affording Ann the rare defence of 'sane automatism'. Howard had told her that he had murdered Rachel because she was blackmailing him. It was better, in any case, than Ann's children knowing that she had intentionally murdered their father in a state of fury and hatred.

And there was Vincent. The principle of 'double jeopardy' was no longer absolute in Queensland. A person could now be tried a second time on the same charge if 'new and compelling' evidence was found and it was 'in the interest of justice'. While Gillian did not think that the DPP would want to prosecute Vincent again, in the light of the fiasco their case had turned into, she did not want to take any chance at all. So Ann could never risk telling anyone what Howard had really said in the kitchen that evening.

Of course, the revelation that Howard was the killer had, at first, caused the ground to shift under Vincent's feet. Was Gillian sure that those were Ann's words? It was unthinkable. Howard was one of the most moral, upstanding people whom you could imagine! And for Rachel Klein to be blackmailing him! He tried to imagine Ann with a knife, actually plunging it through Howard. Did you ever really know another person? Vincent knew also that premeditated murders were rare. Most killers just saw red and lashed out with whatever was at hand, just like Ann. Rachel, however, had obviously been one of the few where the murder was planned carefully. He was also aware that people who do terrible things are often just like everyone else, until the day they cross over into the realm of criminal violence. Then, overnight, they're not like the rest of us at all.

Nothing is what it seems.

The two sets of fingerprints on the glass remained a mystery. The best explanation seemed to be the one mooted in the court, that Vincent's prints had been left on a previous occasion, the glass had merely been rinsed and put away and Howard had drunk from the same glass at a time just prior to the murder. It was just that Vincent couldn't envisage this scenario without Rachel picking up the glass at some point. Oh well, maybe her fingers weren't oily. He tried to put it out of his mind.

Of course, he would have to think of his own future. The partnership couldn't survive this.

Gillian hoped to be briefing Ann's barrister. This might not be possible given the circumstances. But Ann needed to understand the defence that had come to Gillian's mind immediately, on the very evening of Howard's murder. She had to be carefully schooled for exactly what she would say in court, especially for the savage attack the prosecution would have in mind.

Gillian explained to Ann that sane automatism was where the accused had acted involuntarily because of some external cause. The person may have no memory of the event. Under the criminal law, a person cannot be criminally responsible unless the act they had committed is voluntary, done in the exercise of their free will and with the capacity to choose whether or not to act. Under the defence of automatism, it is necessary that it is caused by an external factor and it is unlikely to recur (the public must be protected).

This defence contrasts with that of insane automatism where the automatism is the result of what the court terms 'a disease of the mind', where the violence is prone to recur. If the person is found not guilty because of insanity, he or she is detained in strict security for an indeterminate period of time.

An acquittal on the basis of sane automatism, however, means that the accused walks free.

A notable case in Australia was that of Mary Falconer, a fifty-one-year-old woman who fired a shotgun at close range, killing her estranged husband, who had taunted her about his sexual abuse of two of their daughters. She had telephoned a friend and said she thought she had killed her husband. In interviews with a detective and a psychiatrist, she claimed to have no memory of the act.

In the High Court, the seven judges were agreed that a 'psychological blow' could cause sane automatism. There was no reason to distinguish between psychological and physical trauma. This was the first pronouncement by that court on a case where the automatic behaviour of the accused was alleged to be of psychological origin. The trauma would, however, have to be caused by an 'extraordinary' emotional or mental trauma. If the dissociation were caused by 'ordinary stress', this would suggest insane automatism. Also, it must be the blow alone that caused the dissociation.

The burden of proof would be on the prosecution, who must prove beyond a reasonable doubt that the accused acted voluntarily. Otherwise, that person must be acquitted.

Gillian knew that there was ambivalence in the legal world about automatism being used as a defence. It had even been banned in some jurisdictions. For instance, the distinction in the courts between what was classed as a 'disease of the mind' that manifested itself as violence, and a mental disorder caused by some external factor, was only loosely based on medical knowledge. Who could really decide which of these was prone to recur and which was not?

There was even more skepticism about 'psychological

blow' automatism. It is assumed that it is relatively easy to feign a psychologically-induced state.

However, thanks to Mary Falconer, Gillian was sure that Ann was the perfect candidate. If they reinvented some of the 'facts', that is.

Gillian accompanied Ann to the police interview that morning. Anything she said could be used in evidence against her.

"You admit, Ms Brookes, that you stabbed your husband to death on the night in question?" Detective Winterton asked.

"I can't really admit it, because I have no memory of it," Ann replied. "I only remember looking down at his body. I guess I must have killed him, but I don't remember doing it."

"Do you recall deciding to turn the blade so that the blade was flat?"

"No, of course not. I didn't even know that was the case."

"What *do* you remember of the event, Ms Brookes?"

"I remember my husband telling me something, and after that I seem to have totally sort of blacked out 'til I saw him lying there." Ann was visibly distressed.

"Would you like a break, Ms Brookes?"

"No, I'll be all right, thank you. You can keep going."

"If you're sure. Can you explain 'blacked out' for us? Can you be more specific?" asked the detective.

"All I can say is that there was a period of time that I have no memory of. I still can't remember any of it."

"And what is it that you remember your husband saying to you before you 'blacked out'?"

"He said something terrible. It still shakes me. Do I really have to say?"

"I'm afraid so, Ms Brookes. It is important that we know."

"Well, if I must. He said that it was he who had murdered Rachel Klein. She was blackmailing him. Something about money laundering. But Howard wouldn't have been doing anything dishonest. He was the most moral person you could meet."

"Well, our fraud squad will look into that for us. We don't have anything to do with that side of things. Did he say anything else?"

"No, that's all, as far as I can recall. I think he was just pleading for my help. That's the feeling I had."

"Were you aware that your husband was having an affair with Rachel Klein?" asked Winterton.

"I can't believe that. No. Our marriage was happy and solid. He never cheated on me, not in all those years. Wherever you heard this, it's all vicious gossip and rumour."

"Have you ever been diagnosed with a mental health issue, Ms Brookes?"

"Just depression. Depression and anxiety. Garden variety. Nothing else."

"Did you see a psychiatrist for treatment?" asked Winterton.

"Yes, and still do."

"Do you mind telling us the reason for your depression?"

"Probably the common reason for women. Being tied to the house and children for so many years."

"And did you resent your husband for that?"

"No, of course not. It was a decision we made together. We felt it was the best thing for the children. And Howard was a wonderful provider."

"Have you ever experienced completely losing a period of time, losing memory, prior to this episode?"

"No, never. This has been the only occasion."

The questioning went on, the detective asking Ann the same questions, but in different form. Ann handled the questioning perfectly, Gillian thought.

Memories.

ANN

Next, an appointment was scheduled for a consultation with a state-appointed psychiatrist, Dr Herman Stegmann.

"This is a terrible time for you, Ann. I can't imagine all that you are going through," he said.

"It's beyond words. A true nightmare. I still can hardly believe it. Howard gone. And it seems I killed him. Actually, stabbed him. And what it's done to our children. Their lives have been turned upside down. I don't know if they'll ever forgive me. Even though I didn't mean to do it, can't even remember doing it." Ann began to cry, put her hands over her face.

"I am so sorry, Ann. Just take a few moments when you feel able."

When they resumed, Dr Stegmann began to question Ann.

"I'm sorry Ann, but you do understand that I am going to have to ask you a few questions," he began.

"Yes, I know. That's OK."

"I take it that you have been seeing a psychiatrist for some time. Can you tell me about that?"

"Well, I was fine for several years after the kids were born. I didn't suffer from post-natal depression. But as they got older, just looking after them and the house, well I started to feel as if something was missing. I didn't go to university when I finished school and would have liked to enrol as a mature aged student. I guess that's why I started getting depressed," Ann answered. "That's what my therapist thinks anyway."

"And why was it that you weren't able to take up study at some stage?" asked Dr Stegmann.

"Well, Howard and I had both agreed that it would be best for the children if I stayed at home with them. He works long hours and he wanted to go up the ladder. But once the kids were both at school, I didn't think I needed to be at home full-time."

"And your husband didn't agree? He didn't want you to pursue a career?"

"No. He thought the children would need my support through secondary school. And he liked me to organise dinner parties for clients. He thought he earned enough. And we were well off."

"And you resented him for that?"

"No. Of course not. How could I resent him? He was a wonderful husband. I had everything I could ask for. I just wished he could have seen things from a different point of view. But he just wanted what was best for all of us as a family unit. And I was about to start a uni course soon, as it happened."

"Did your husband know about this?"

"No. As a matter of fact, I was just about to tell him."

"Can you remember clearly the conversation you were having with Howard prior to your loss of memory?"

"Yes, it's strange. I felt as if I was detached from the situation, as if I were just an observer. And yet I do remember what Howard was saying."

"Can you tell me what he *was* saying to you? Are you able to talk about it?"

"Yes, I had to tell the police. It was just awful. He said

that he had murdered Rachel Klein, that she was blackmailing him, something to do with money laundering."

"Can you remember how you were feeling as he was telling you all of this? Shocked? Angry?"

"No, I don't remember anything except having a sense of watching on from a distance. Nothing seemed real. And after that, I don't remember anything until I was looking down at Howard's body. And then I guess what I was feeling was shock and disbelief."

"On the questionnaire you had described briefly a traumatic event from your childhood, seeing your brother being run over and killed by a car."

"Yes, that is so."

"And what was your reaction to that? What do you recall?"

"Well, I was only young too. I remember extreme grief and stress. Crying. Staying in my room. Not wanting to go to school. Mum and Dad took me to a psychologist for a long time."

"Did you experience any violent reaction at the time of the accident?"

"No, nothing. I was old enough that I would remember. My parents never mentioned anything."

"And what about in later life? Have you ever felt violent tendencies towards anyone?"

"No, and I don't have nightmares about it either. I'm not self-destructive. I don't self-isolate. Doctor, I know something of the symptoms of PTSD, and I don't suffer from it. My psychiatrist ruled that out right from the start. I am happy for you to consult with her."

When the session was over, Gillian picked Ann up and took her home to discuss the situation. They could not go somewhere for a coffee or wine as the coronavirus lockdown had started. Vincent and Gillian had fitted in their celebratory dinner at Montrechet just in time.

The Queensland justice system, though, had not shut down. It was moving along, slowly and relentlessly, just as it always did.

To Ann, the restrictions, closures and social distancing meant little. She had no desire to see anyone. Even seeing her children was heart-rending. They had not shunned her, but any meeting with them was understandably uneasy. Their father was dead. Their mother had killed him, brutally, violently. They had stopped going to university and had moved into a rented apartment together.

Vincent and Gillian were helping Ann with the sale of her home. It would be difficult to sell. It had become famous, an attraction. People liked to drive by and point it out. Nobody wanted to live in a murder house. It would only sell to some adventurous soul, at a greatly reduced price. Then the three of them would look for an apartment for Ann, and another for her children. Ann had little interest in any of it. Her mind was now consumed by fear of what she faced in a courtroom, and she kept reliving Howard telling her that he was going to leave her, wanted someone who arose passion in him. She was glad he was dead and glad that Rachel was too.

But now she would be spending her life alone. She had lost her treasured home. Her relationship with her children would be forever changed. Friends kept her at arm's length. But, in spite of all this, she did not want to go to jail.

She and Gillian talked over the consultation with the psychiatrist.

"You were right, Gillian," Ann said. "He did seem to be

heading towards PTSD."

"Yes, as I said, that way the prosecution could establish insane automatism, what courts call 'a disease of the mind' or an *internal* cause. That way you can be locked away in strict security, though not in a jail, for an indeterminate period of time. We'll be arguing 'sane automatism', where the automatism is caused by trauma, in other words an *external* cause. The prosecution won't go ahead with the insane option now. They won't have sufficient grounds. They will try to establish intent to murder but we have the perfect defence."

"No, I told the doctor today that my own psychiatrist long ago ruled out PTSD. Probably because of the intensive therapy I had at the time, after my brother's death.

"And the courts do not accept depression as a 'disease of the mind'. That's because it's such a familiar condition. Most members of the jury have either experienced it or know someone who has. So the prosecution can't use that as an external cause. They'll be trying to prove intent to kill. But we'll get you acquitted using our defence."

Killing lies.

ANN

The media revelled in the scandal. Ann was a talking point, a psychopath, deranged, mentally unstable. She was analysed, in the media, by those who once had been her friends or Howard's, and over the dinner tables of people who had never met her. Everyone had an opinion. It was always the quiet ones, those who knew her said. It was her age, the menopause, others claimed. Knowing heads nodded. Had you heard that she had been the only one to see her younger brother die? Who knows — maybe she had pushed him in front of that car? Some people were just born bad. Who knew what else she had done? She had never had to work a day in her life. Her husband had worked night and day to keep her in the style she was accustomed to. No wonder he had started seeing someone else. And she was sure to plead insanity to get away with it.

Gillian had extricated Ann from all social media. Vincent had come to accept that she had not known what she was doing at the time. He saw the repercussions she and her children were having to suffer, and gave Gillian his support in helping her through it. He could not be privy to Ann's confidential sessions with Gillian as her lawyer, but could see where their defence would be heading.

Gillian introduced her to Hilary who was non-judgmental and even understanding. They bonded through the experience of rejection. Gillian and Vincent had managed to find a buyer for Ann's home. The sale did not seem to affect her much. She appeared to have detached from it, in light of what it now represented, a life that was no more and the site of so much pain. Gillian and Vincent had found a pleasant but unpretentious apartment for Ann in a highly-secured and private complex in Teneriffe. She would be using an assumed name with the building managers and committee and any other resident she might encounter. A lawyer friend had discreetly handled the transactions for them. Ann would be venturing out as little as possible. Until the coronavirus scare had dissipated, no one was permitted to socialise in any case.

As it happened, in the latter months as the situation improved, restrictions eased. Sometime away at Noosa gave Ann a little relief, as she was less likely to be recognised there, and she and Gillian could go out a little. They knew that the media would be doing all in its power to steal photographs of Ann and all movements had to be made carefully.

Hilary joined them at times on weekends. Ann wanted to buy somewhere for her children also, and she was liaising with them about that too, attempting to secure them more privacy. They also lacked enthusiasm.

The weight that Ann felt pressing down on her was large and relentless. While Gillian continued to reassure her about what a great argument they could present, the idea of proving whether what she had done was voluntary or not seemed to her, extremely subjective and uncertain. She tried to push thoughts of prison and imaginings of what it would be like, how she would be old when she got out, whether her children would even want to visit her, to the back of her mind. She had no choice but to get on with it and intrusive thoughts just made that harder.

She was not the first to wonder how life had sunk so low, when she seemingly had everything.

Of course, she had engaged a barrister, and with Vincent free of the court system, it had been possible for Gillian to brief him. Together, they prepared Ann and rehearsed her for everything that the courtroom could throw at her.

And today, here they were again, for the second time this year, in the confines of the Supreme Court of Queensland. It was impossible to not be in awe of the raw power implicit in these environs. When a decision was brought down here a defendant was powerless to ignore it or refuse to obey. Democracy was certainly demonstrated through rule of law and natural justice, the right of both parties to present their case. But once the verdict was brought down, the sentence pronounced, the only avenue left was the Court of Appeal, and by leave only, the High Court. And that was the very end of the road.

The judge instructed the jury on matters of law such as the presumption and standard of proof, and the burden of proof, and impressed on them that a person cannot be criminally responsible unless the action that they have committed has been voluntary, that they have been able to choose whether to act or not.

Mr B.J Simmons, SC, for the prosecution, in his opening statement, brought to the jury's attention that the facts were clear. A man had turned to his wife in despair, confessing, she said, to a murder. The action of a reasonable person would have been, should have been, to have rung triple zero. Instead, she had viciously stabbed him to death. The defence would have the jury believe that the shock, the psychological blow that she had received, was so extreme as to cause her to enter into a dissociative state, in which she was not capable of controlling her actions. The prosecution would show that there was not a sufficient degree of likelihood that the accused had been dissociated and not responsible for her actions. Rather, they would show that the accused had acted in a fury, using the knife in her hands to kill her husband in cold blood. She had learned that very afternoon that he had been seeing another woman. That was the logical explanation. There was generally no basis in criminal offences for doubting that an accused was capable of controlling his or her actions. The prosecution would demonstrate that here, the defendant had worked herself into a frenzy, something that she did have control over, something we all have control over. In fact, they would show that there was a degree of deliberateness in the act that left no doubt that she was in control of her actions and that she intended to kill.

So, the prosecution argued intent to kill. The accused had been subject to trauma. They had no argument with that. But had that trauma been so great that the ordinary person would be unlikely to have withstood it? Examination of the facts purported to show the jury that the answer was unquestionably 'no'.

Their first expert witness, a psychiatrist, described the phenomenon of dissociation and under what circumstances it can occur. The precedent case of Mary Falconer, which established 'psychological blow' automatism in Australia, was contrasted with the case now before the court. In the precedent case, two psychiatrists were prepared to agree that Mary Falconer had entered a dissociative state in response to taunting by her estranged husband. There was a major difference, however, from the present case. The things Mr

Falconer said, which led his wife to pick up a rifle and shoot him, recalled and taunted her about his sexual abuse of their daughters, led her to believe that the court would not believe these allegations, terrified her about the future and caused her to realise for the first time, that he had also sexually abused their foster daughter.

In other words, Mary Falconer had heard a direct threat to her children. Her children had been severely harmed and may be again, and they may soon face their case being disbelieved in the court. Nothing could be more traumatic to a mother than the threat of sexual and physical harm to her children.

By contrast, the words spoken to Ann Brookes by her husband conveyed no direct threat to her children, physical or sexual, nor to her. They implied a consequence to her husband, if he or she chose to do the right thing and report the crime. They may have implied lifestyle change and harm to reputation. But these were all possibilities that were arrived at through a person contemplating the situation over a period of time. They would involve decisions to be made. They were by no means the same as the sudden realisation by Mary Falconer that her children were in immediate danger.

Howard Brookes' words would not have provoked dissociation but simply rage at the lie they had been living as a married couple. While a person might not generally be responsible for entering into dissociative states, like sleepwalking or concussion, where deliberative functions of the mind might be said to be absent, this could not be said of a person who worked herself into an emotional frenzy.

The prosecution therefore distinguished the case of Mary Falconer.

In addition, a forensic expert testified that the carving

knife which had been the murder weapon, had been plunged into the victim's rib cage with the blade horizontal. This is how it had been able to enter the body of the deceased between his ribs, puncturing his lungs so that he drowned in his own blood. This could only be seen as a deliberate angling of the knife, a calculated act, and therefore a voluntary one under the control of the accused's will.

That Ms Ann Brookes had intended to kill her husband Howard Brooks was beyond reasonable doubt.

Words.

ANN

The defence had to come back strongly to establish lack of volition, that what Ann Brookes did, was physically uncontrollable, and therefore, the defence of sane automatism. To do this, they had to leave the jury with no reasonable doubt that she had entered a dissociative state as a reaction to an extraordinary psychological blow.

They attacked the prosecution's claim that the blow or trauma could not be compared to that suffered in Mary Falconer's case. Even the prosecution had not attempted to dispute that the accused had suffered trauma. It would be difficult to imagine that hearing your spouse admit to a brutal murder would not have a profound effect on any reasonable person. Undoubtedly, Howard Brookes had delivered an extraordinary blow. While that suffered by Mary Falconer might have suggested a sexual and physical threat to her children, that inflicted on Ann Brookes posed a huge psychological and emotional threat. She would see their lives ruined through scandal, and the shame and sense of loss her children would suffer through knowing that their father whom they had always believed to be decent and moral and normal, was actually a cold-blooded killer. And who can say how long these thoughts would take to run through a person's mind? It may be only a fraction of a second.

Certainly though, it was not difficult to imagine trauma of

such magnitude causing a dissociative state in a normal person. Dissociation as explained by their expert psychiatrist, is a natural reaction to feelings about experiences that the individual cannot control. This was indisputably the case here. While not every person of sound mind, dissociates every time extraordinary trauma occurs, a disproportionate number do.

He explained 'disaster syndrome' where during a disaster, though not physically affected, people wandered aimlessly, seemingly unaware of their surroundings. Ordinary people can dissociate in response to severe trauma.

Ann's psychiatrist, Dr Susan Mathews, given a partial waiver of confidentiality, testified that Ann did not exhibit any of the symptoms associated with PTSD. This was in spite of her traumatic childhood experience, and probably because of expert therapy at the time. She found her to be the most rational and resilient of people. The depression she had treated Ann for was experienced by many, and did not interfere with day-to-day function.

The forensic witness for the defence gave testimony. She addressed the angle of the knife. She illustrated for the jury a re-enactment of the situation where a person could be slicing into something, such as a piece of meat, with the blade vertical, then turn it at ninety degrees as they turned and thrust the knife. It was quite natural for the knife also, without any conscious will, to now be horizontal to the floor. It was not necessary, as the prosecution had argued, for the person holding it to make a deliberate decision to turn the knife through ninety degrees.

Ann took the stand. The jury, her barrister said, would want to hear from her own lips what had occurred, just as she told him. She couldn't have presented more convincingly as far as a jury was concerned. Her appearance did not scream 'money'. She was quiet and reserved, self-effacing. For once, she got it right with her clothes she chose for court. She was dressed in a simple blue and white shirt dress coupled with white pumps. Her only embellishment was a single strand of beads. Her hair was short, flecks of grey beginning to appear. She wore little makeup, as always. She was the very embodiment of middle-class.

Who in that courtroom, Gillian thought, could have imagined her to be a cold-blooded, calculating murderess?

And they had schooled her well. That was always essential when the accused was to take the stand. No defence lawyer would ever forget Lindy Chamberlain being condemned in the court of public opinion. She was found guilty because 'you could just tell'. She was too unemotional, too undemonstrative, too stoic. No mother would act like that.

Ann had to be a more sympathetic figure. She could not be so emotional as to appear false. Nor could she seem cold. In fact, this was not a difficult role for Ann. She was, naturally, suffering greatly from grief. She had, after all, lost everything that she held dear. On the other hand, she was not given to public displays of emotion. She could walk the middle road asked of her. On the stand, she appeared terribly sad but not histrionic.

She was, however, prepared to do all she could to secure her freedom. That was all she had now. She would follow all the instructions her lawyers had given her in regard to what she was about to face in the courtroom.

"Ms Brookes, can you tell us how long you and your late husband had been married?" her lawyer began.

"Yes, we had been married for twenty-two years in April this year." Her eyes were clear and steady, her voice soft and controlled.

"And would you say that your marriage had been a happy one?"

"Yes, very. We had brought up two wonderful children. Had created a beautiful home. Enjoy holidays and outings together regularly."

"Were you familiar with Rachel Klein before her alleged murder?"

"Only superficially. She was a paralegal in the practice, of course, and we had met on a couple of occasions at work functions. But very briefly."

"Do you recall your husband making particular mention of Ms Klein in the weeks leading up to her death?"

"Not at all. I don't remember Howard *ever* mentioning her, in fact. She wasn't *his* paralegal."

"So you were surprised when he brought up her name when he came home that night."

"I was more than surprised. Considering what he told me about her, I was shocked beyond belief.

"And what was it that he said about Ms Klein?"

"He told me…" And here she faltered, dropping her eyes to look at her hands. She looked up again. "He said that he was the one who killed her."

"And did he say why he had killed Rachel Klein?"

"He said that she had been blackmailing him. Over money laundering, he said. I remember that clearly, though it didn't make any sense."

"How did you feel on learning that?"

"Well, you might imagine. I don't think any word can describe it. Shocked. Bewildered. Nothing made sense any more. Nothing was real. The world was off its axis."

Ann appeared at this point to be talking to herself, to have forgotten where she was. Her defence lawyer refocused her attention.

"And what happened next, Ms Brookes?"

Ann seemed to drag her attention back to proceedings at hand.

"That's just it. I don't know what happened. I just can't remember. I can't remember anything after hearing Howard tell me the terrible thing he had done."

The court was completely silent, rapt, no one wanting to miss a word.

"What is the first thing you *do* remember?"

"I remember looking down at Howard's body. I knew he was dead. It was clear that he was dead."

Murmurs now rose from the courtroom. This was the crux of the matter. Would spectators believe it? More importantly, would the jury believe it?

"What did you do next?"

"Well, I don't know exactly when, but I rang Gillian, Gillian Barnwell."

"And why did you ring Gillian?"

"She is my closest friend. I was shocked, confused. I needed a friend. This was all outside my experience. I can't really explain. It was my first impulse."

"What time did your husband arrive that evening, Ms Brookes?"

"It was around six."

"And did you open the front door to let him in?"

No, he did what he always did, let himself in and came straight through to the kitchen. He usually found me there when he got home. And that night our two children were coming over for dinner."

"And what exactly, were you doing when he came into the kitchen?"

"I was slicing an eye fillet into steaks."

"Thank you , Ms Brookes."

"That's all Your Honour."

Fiction has to make sense. Truth doesn't.

ANN

The worst, of course, was yet to come.

After an adjournment, the cross began.

"Ms Brookes, on the afternoon of this particular day of your husband's death, a revelation regarding your husband came to light in the case of Vincent Barnwell, did it not?"

"Yes, that is so."

"And what was that revelation, Ms Brookes?"

"That my husband's fingerprints had been found on a glass in Rachel Klein's house."

"Ms Klein being the victim of the alleged murder?"

"Yes, that is correct."

"And you were aware that your husband had been to Ms Klein's home?"

"No, I was not. Not until that moment."

"Were you, Ms Brookes, in the courtroom at the time?"

"Yes. Yes I was."

"And can you describe what went through your mind at that moment?"

Ann hesitated. "I can't really say. It was so unexpected. Such a shock. I suppose I was just confused."

"Did it occur to you that perhaps it was your husband who had committed the crime, not the defendant Vincent Brookes?"

"No, of course not. That did not even enter my mind."

"Are you sure of that? Was that something you

considered? Even for a second? So that perhaps it was not quite the shock you imagined, when your husband came home later that day?"

"Objection! Your Honour, the question has been asked and answered." From Ann's lawyer.

"Quite so. Move on, Mr Simmons."

"Did it cross your mind then that your husband had been at Rachel Klein's home because he was having an affair with her?"

"No, I know — knew - Howard too well for that. He had never been unfaithful to me. No, to answer your question, I did not think of that."

"Oh come, Ms Brookes, do you want the jury to believe that, when you learned that your husband had been to a young woman's home and had not told you, you did not even consider that he was having more than just a work relationship?"

"No, I did not think that."

"So, on hearing about the fingerprints on a glass, a wine glass to be exact, you did not feel at all angry or jealous and work yourself into a fury before the victim came home after work? So angry by then, that you killed him out of sheer rage?"

"No, that was not the case."

"Do you really expect the jury…?"

"Objection! Your Honour, Mr Simmons is badgering the witness."

"Sustained. Mr Simmons, you have been warned."

"Yes, Your Honour. Ms Brookes, had you been aware of the blackmail that Mr Brookes confessed to you?"

"No, he had not told me about it before."

"So, how do you think Ms Klein had found out about it? Might it have been a case of pillow talk?"

"Objection. Calls for speculation."

"Sustained."

"So, you were not aware of a large credit card payment to Tiffany's for the purchase of very expensive jewellery?"

"No, I was not aware of that. Howard was the one who checked the credit card statements."

"This was a joint account, was it not?"

"Still, I didn't usually look at it. Howard used to look after all of that."

"I gather you were not, yourself, the recipient of this valuable jewellery?"

"No. It was probably to do with the blackmail he told me about."

"So, you had not previously become aware of the purchase, and harboured resentment and jealousy, so the fingerprint revelation was the tipping point?"

"No, as I said, I knew nothing about any jewellery."

"I put to you that a combination of festering jealousy, together with the suddenly acquired knowledge of the fingerprints on a wine glass at Rachel Klein's home, pushed you to the brink. So that when your husband came home on that fateful day, you could not contain your anger and jealousy any longer. And *that* is why you killed your husband."

"No, that was not the case. I was not feeling jealousy or anger. I was just shocked when Howard told me what he had done. I've told you all this."

"Phone records for that afternoon show that your husband attempted to phone you three times but you did not answer. Can you explain why you did not answer?"

"I guess I just needed time to think everything over. What I had heard in the courtroom came out of left field. I wanted to roll it over for a while before he came home. It's difficult to explain."

"Yes, it's difficult to explain because it is not what happened. You did not want to answer you husband's calls because you were extremely angry with him and wanted him to stew, and so your anger just kept festering 'til he came home."

"Objection, Your Honour. My colleague is badgering again."

"Sustained. I will not warn you again. Mr Simmons, proceed."

Simmons turned back to Ann.

"You have described for us the first thing you remember after coming back to reality. That was the sight of your husband lying dead on the floor, knife still protruding from his body. Is that an accurate representation?"

Ann visibly flinched. She took a big breath and exhaled.

"Yes, that is the first thing I remember."

"And the first thing that occurred to you to do was not, say, ring triple zero, or even one of your children, but in fact, your first instinct was to phone a criminal defence lawyer. Is that correct, Ms Brookes?"

"Yes, but…"

"I have no further questions, Your Honour."

Ann was barely able to attend to the remainder of the trial. How had she done? Had she made things better or worse? Would it have been better had she not taken the stand?

The closing argument for the defence, however, brought things back into focus for her. He reminded the jury of the magnitude of the shock she had suffered, trauma of such magnitude that, he was sure the jury could imagine, most people would not be able to withstand. It was exactly the kind of traumatic event that was typically linked with dissociative states, as described by their psychiatrist, a natural reaction to experiences that individuals cannot control.

He reminded them of the Mary Falconer case and of the parallels with this one and its relevance. He reminded them also that no evidence had been presented that illustrated that Ann had been angry or jealous because of the revelation in the Vincent Barnwell trial, certainly not the degree of anger required to decide to kill, to commit cold, premeditated murder. Finally, Ann had rung Gillian Barnwell, not because she was her lawyer, but because she was her best friend.

The judge then directed the jury on matters of law.

The jury retired to consider their verdict.

The waiting seemed interminable.

Ann spent the time with Gillian. They had a few wines. Who knew if this might be Ann's last chance to have a wine, for who knows how long? This question remained unspoken, but hung in the air.

Gillian ordered in food, but Ann could only pick at it. God only knew how death row prisoners managed to eat their last meal.

At the beginning, Ann obsessed. She knew it was futile but wanted an answer from Gillian. Would the jury find her guilty or not guilty? She sought reassurance. Gillian did her best but could not tell her what she wanted to hear. Finally, Ann gave up.

She spoke to her children on the phone. They wished her well but they were despondent and their voices strained. What must it be like for them, one parent dead and the other charged with his murder, possibly about to go to prison for a long time?

She thought about the jury. Seven had been women. Would they feel sorry for her, believing her to be either a jealous woman scorned in favour of a beautiful much younger woman or one who had received a terrible blow of a different kind? Would they believe the killing to have been committed deliberately, in fury, or unknowingly, while in some sort of a trance?

The day came to an end with no word of a verdict. They found it almost impossible to get any sleep.

They were back in court the next morning.

Finally, word came. The jury had reached a verdict.

Ann had seen this scene played out on television and at the movies. All stood for the judge. The jury streamed in. Were they avoiding looking at her?

Ann was asked to stand.

Madam Foreman and Members of the Jury, have you agreed upon your verdict?"

"Yes, we have."

On a charge of murder, a verdict has to to be unanimous.

"How say you on the charge of murder? Do you find Ann Brooks guilty or not guilty?"

Ann felt now as if this time she *had* dissociated, that she was not really present, but was merely looking in as an observer. She heard the words as if from afar, as if they had nothing to do with her.

"We find the defendant… not guilty."

Ann was free to go.

Thank you, Mary.

The media had revelled in the trial. They had whipped the public into a frenzy. Everyone had an opinion. It mattered not that they had not been in the courtroom, had not seen or heard any of the witnesses. It was the now the all too familiar 'trial by media'.

Now that the 'not guilty' verdict had come in, the public were even more frenzied. The most common view voiced around dining tables or on social media was that it was 'all a load of bullshit'! Nobody committed murder because they were 'out of their mind' for a few minutes and didn't know what they were doing. Most had never heard the word 'automatism', but everyone was now an expert. Trust a lawyer to come up with that. It was always the same. There was one law for the rich, and one for the rest of us.

Strangely, few doubted that 'the bastard' had killed Rachel Klein. Few questioned that he had been laundering money, whatever that actually meant. No, if an ordinary bloke stole ten bucks he'd be in jail. But these wealthy, white-collar criminals, who knew how many of them were stashing millions away. If you knew the right people!

Of course, women generally had little sympathy for Rachel Klein. They had followed her activities throughout Vincent's trial. How many women's husbands had she been involved with? All rich, naturally, a real gold digger. And blackmail, as well! She had asked for it.

And so it went on. There seemed, as usual, to be little faith in the legal process or the verdict. What *is* justice anyway, when one cold-blooded murderer kills another?

And there was talk that Ann Brookes would now be getting her husband's life insurance on top of everything. Apparently he was insured for some huge amount. How could that be? She was the one who had killed him. The 'not guilty' verdict did not come into it, as far as the general public were concerned, it seemed. Ann, of course, verdict or not, was allowed no private life. Gillian helped her change her mobile phone number, but going out for any reason had become a nightmare. The press were camped at both gates to her complex. She could neither sneak out on foot nor drive out of her carpark without being mobbed.

Gillian and Hilary were her only visitors, although she sometimes visited Gillian and Vincent at their home or her children at theirs. At first, Vincent found the horrifying death of Howard hard to contemplate but now that he had absorbed the fact that it had happened, he had developed a kind of sympathy for Ann. Why Howard had not just brought the blackmail into the open, instead of committing murder, was almost impossible to fathom. But Howard *had* been extremely proud. Arrogant even. His reputation had been central to his existence. And he, Vincent, knew how one could come to hate Rachel. And he, like Ann, knew too well what it was like to be charged with murder, wait for an interminable length of time and then sit in a courtroom watching the faces of a jury and hoping, praying to God, for a 'not guilty' verdict. Also, in a perverse way, it may have been thanks to Ann that he now had his freedom.

Ann's children knew that they would always suffer from their mother's actions, but in a way, it was all because of their father. He had pushed their mother to breaking point. And their father's expectations *had* always been difficult to live up to. For them *and* their mother. Things were still a little strained between them and Ann, but were softening a little.

Ann, Gillian and Hilary were, almost imperceptibly, drawing closer as a group, bound by an invisible thread of shared rejection. Ann did not admit to Hilary that Howard had rejected her, though of course Gillian knew, and Hilary guessed at it. If Ann had felt an irresistible impulse to kill her husband, to Hilary it was motivated by one thing and one thing only — he no longer wanted her. She knew because of the urge she had herself experienced — the overwhelming desire to kill Phil. She had felt a hatred she had not known possible and she was sure Ann had too. And because of this, she felt an unspoken empathy.

There was something both Hilary and Ann believed but did not, out of respect for Gillian, speak of. This was a certainty that she, also, had been wronged by Vincent but would never say. His having been going back to Rachel Klein's house after hours, just to finish up work? Having a wine with her? Someone who looked like that? No matter that it had not been proven in court of law, they were quite certain of the reason Vincent was at her apartment and that was because he and Rachel were lovers. If Michelle Hildebrand had been questioned, on a second day in court, and the judge had allowed her to reveal Rachel's confidences, that would surely have emerged — as, Hilary was sure, Howard Brookes' relationship with Rachel would also have been revealed. But it was all water under the bridge now, as they say. Their suffering had been extreme but they now had the strongest of compacts with each other. They knew that each one of them would be there for the other two.

Ann did not return to Dr Matthews, not even to thank her. She knew that the psychiatrist would probably deduce that she had *not* been in a dissociative state, that she did not want an expert to probe her about any of that. But Ann did not care whether or not the doctor guessed at her guilt. She had opened a new chapter in her life and she had wanted to leave her past as far behind as possible. Besides, she could never be tried again for Howard's murder, not without compelling new evidence. And Dr Matthews did not, and would never, have such proof. As for her barrister, if Ann wished, she could tell him straight to his face that she had murdered her husband knowingly, and in cold blood, because he could do nothing either. He was bound by lawyer–client privilege.

Ann felt stronger than she had in a long time.

I'm still standing.

PART THREE

HOW IT ALL ENDED

HILARY

The conversations among Gillian, Ann and Hilary were, in the beginning, benign. They tried to diverge from the obvious discourse, the monotonous events that had been occupying their lives recently.

Small-talk centred on the coronavirus, the rise of unemployment, the businesses that had not reopened, in particular local restaurants and cafes. Overseas travel was less popular. The world had changed, seemingly overnight.

They talked of investments, of the stock market, of effects on superannuation and property prices. Ann was to come into a very large amount of money, courtesy of Howard's generous life insurance policy. Of course, she would have her children's university fees and living expenses and the cost of a car for each for a start. She would still have money to invest but nothing seemed certain.

Ann's plans for university study were well and truly on hold. She could not imagine ever putting herself into such a public forum as the University of Queensland. On-line study? It just did not quite seem the same, not the experience she had dreamed of. Maybe in time.

However, Hilary could not help but come back to her situation from time to time. In some ways, she felt, Gillian's and Ann's problem circumstances were now resolved, no matter how dreadful the process had been. Gillian was now living as normal a life as possible after Vincent enduring a murder trial. But they did have each other and seemed at peace. Ann did not have a partner, but she was not having to suffer her husband's rejection of her and his infidelity; whereas she, Hilary, was having to watch on while her husband paraded his infidelity with his new, young lover before the whole world. Hilary herself seemed to be a social pariah, no longer invited to the dinner parties she had once enjoyed as one half of a couple. She also had to endure the knowledge that the one who accompanied Phil to these occasions would be a suntanned (fake), pouty-lipped (filler), eyelash-extended (false), flaxen maned (artificial) beauty named, of all things, Kendall. How young she was. There was nothing quite like youth, Hilary knew, no substitute for the 'real' thing.

She would be the recipient of a very decent property settlement. However, down the track Phil and Kendall would marry and would no doubt have a child (Kendall's insurance). Hilary could just see the future now. Phil dying. All his possessions going to Kendall and her offspring and none to Hilary's children. It happened every day. She could not bear to think about it. Whereas if something happened to Kendall now, well she doubted that he had changed his will yet, they had not lived together for the requisite time, and she, Hilary, *was* still his wife. She knew all about Kendall, who was prolific on social media. From her photos, she seemed almost a child. She worked as a personal trainer, three days a week. She was a fitness junkie, hence her lean, tanned body. She jogged, ponytail swinging. She ran marathons and trained assiduously for them.

Hilary could not get all these thoughts out of her mind.

The psychologist she saw talked about thought distortions. Fortune telling — her children would miss out on their inheritance. Black and white thinking — you were only attractive to a man if you were young and thin. Catastrophising — her life was ruined. The psychologist encouraged her to challenge her thoughts and reframe them. It was not, apparently, what happened to you, but how you dealt with it. It was normal to suffer grief after such a huge loss of expectation. Hilary *would* reach the desired stage of 'acceptance'. She would not be stuck forever in the 'blame' and 'anger' stages. Blah, blah, blah. White noise. Couldn't anyone understand that what she was experiencing was simply anger and resentment, that any normal woman would feel when abandoned for a younger woman? Nothing 'distorted' about it at all.

But was it normal to wish Kendall dead? Hilary didn't ask.

She spoke to her two friends about it. Gillian wondered if there was some way that Hilary could avenge herself on the young interloper. How much did Hilary know about her?

"Maybe we should look into her past. There may be something there that could be used to harm her, her reputation, her fitness business. You never know. Might be worth a try," suggested Gillian.

"I guess so. It's a bit of a long shot. How do we go about it, though?"

I have an investigator friend that I use sometimes. Ill get him to look into it."

When that avenue proved fruitless, all three began recording Kendall's weekly activities and movements on social media sites. She stuck almost obsessively to a routine. For example, she spent every Wednesday training for her precious marathons, the first Wednesday of every month being a hike up a Mount Barney trail. She would set off very early in the morning and return just before dark. The trail was lonely during the week. Now, if two people were waiting on her return descent trip along the track, the one she did not recognise sitting near the edge of a vertical drop with an ankle injury, the other hiding ready to shove, what might eventuate?

The thought festered.

Gillian and Hilary would need to familiarise themselves with the trail and start some serious training and research.

The first newspaper account was on 27th October.

MISSING HIKER FEARED LOST

A Brisbane hiker who failed to return yesterday afternoon is now the subject of an intensive search by Queensland Fire and Emergency Services.

It is believed that twenty-seven-year-old Kendall O'Brien may have become disorientated while hiking in Mt Barney National Park south of Brisbane. In addition to her becoming disorientated, it seems that the battery of the mobile phone the hiker was carrying may have run out.

The trailhead is located at the base of Mt Barney on Barney View Road. There the Upper Portal track leads to the Mt Maroon summit.

Rescue crews began their search early this morning. The massive operation includes twenty-six people, helicopters and K-9 units.

The missing woman was last seen yesterday morning at her home in Brisbane's inner north.

"She is passionate about her fitness and loves her hiking on Mt Barney," her partner said.

A spokesman for Queensland Parks and Wildlife Services warned that summit routes were suitable only for well-prepared hikers, with a high level of fitness and bush navigation skills. "Hikers should never attempt the climb alone," he said.

Gillian, Hilary and Ann could have told the rescuers exactly where Kendall O'Brien was and that if she had become disorientated, it was because she had fallen over the edge of a steep embankment until her long drop had finally been broken by a rocky outcrop.

The searchers were soon to find this out for themselves. It was reported on 30th October.

HIKER FOUND DEAD IN MT BARNEY NATIONAL PARK

A twenty-seven -year-old woman who went missing in Mt Barney National Park has been found dead.

Rescuers found the body of Kendall O'Brien lying on rocks at the foot of a steep embankment on a summit track popular with dedicated hikers.

A police spokesman said that the woman is believed to have arrived at the trailhead around 7.30 a.m. on 26th October.

Her partner reported her missing at around 8 p.m. that night, when she failed to return home. He had tried calling her but she did not answer.

A search team of twenty-six, comprising police, fire and rescue personnel, SES representatives and other volunteers along with dogs, helicopters and drones equipped with thermal imagery, scoured the area surrounding the track.

They found the body at around 2 p.m. yesterday.

"At this point we do not suspect foul play," the spokesman added. He said that an autopsy would determine cause of death.

"It's a hazardous area," he said. "We have no idea why she would have wandered two metres off the track itself. She must have slipped and fallen."

Her brother, Sean O'Brien, said that she was an experienced hiker.

"She's someone who's done marathons, triathlons. You name it — she's done it. She's really sporty and picks up new skills quickly," he said.

That would have been the end of it. However, sometimes the stars just all align.

It just so happened, it emerged later, that Kendall had not taken her phone with her on that fateful day. She had forgotten to charge it. She left it behind in her handbag and decided to take Phil's just in case something went wrong. She had left Phil sleeping. *(Location finder history.)*

On top of that, Phil had not gone to work that day. He wanted to work on his house plans for a client at home on his drafting desk, alone and undisturbed. He also, ironically, wanted to think about wriggling out of this relationship with Kendall. It had become tedious. *She* had become tedious, all this obsessive exercising and training, never a decent meal on the table at the end of the day, chirpy 'conversation' about her athletic progress, evenings glued to Snapchat. He found himself wishing he were free of her. *(No alibi.)*

And to put the icing on the cake, a lot was known about ballistics now, and how bodies behave in mid-air. Someone falling from a height has a different trajectory downward from someone who was pushed. *(Forensics.)*

The only hikers who came forward, two young men, said they could remember passing a couple, a man and a woman, on the track that day but no, they did not take much notice of what they looked like. *(Witnesses.)*

Not knowing any of this, Gillian, Hilary and Ann were taken aback to read a news article which began —

DEATH OF MT BARNEY HIKER SUSPICIOUS

Police are questioning a man in relation to the death of a woman in the Mt Barney National Park recently
   The body of Kendall O'Brien was found……

Oh Phil. Remember the old saying.

Be careful what you wish for.

www.ingramcontent.com/pod-product-compliance
Lightning Source LLC
LaVergne TN
LVHW091537060526
838200LV00036B/641